Landfall

Julius Horwitz

Landfall

HOLT, RINEHART and WINSTON
New York

Published simultaneously in Canada by Holt, Rinehart and Winston of Canada, Limited.

Library of Congress Cataloging in Publication Data
Horwitz, Julius, 1920–
  Landfall.
  I. Title.
PZ4.H8244Lan [PS3558.0728]   813'.5'4   76–29904
ISBN 0–03–014926–6

First Edition

Published in the United States of America
10 9 8 7 6 5 4 3 2 1

To Lois, Jon, and David

Moreover, something is or seems
That touches me with mystic gleams,
Like glimpses of forgotten dreams—

Of something felt, like something here;
Of something done, I know not where;
Such as no language may declare.

TENNYSON

One

Elaine

When I sail I seem to know why I was born and why I live. The sea is clean no matter what the ecologists tell you. Even the Long Island Sound has the look of a bright clear morning at the dawn of the world. My boat moves through the water with ease. The sails respond to the wind and my touch. Nothing has changed in five thousand years. The boatmen of ancient Egypt and Phoenicia sailed this way and certainly the Chinese in the South China seas made their way by sail from coast to coast. No one knows when the sail was born just as no one knows when we were born. All of us now come into a fully made world, or so we think until night overtakes us and we begin the wild sleep of dreams when we don't know which world we inhabit. I find the water comforting. I take the sailboat out alone. I am grateful to my husband for insisting that I learn to sail. It was perhaps the one unselfish act between us that I can attribute to him. My husband is an American man, he seems to want me to retain the individuality of a housefly.

I have fooled him. God knows how I have fooled him. I have terrible dreams. I have bright, brilliant daydreams. I see sunsets no one in Larchmont has ever seen from their sun porches. I smile like a child of five who still sees the wonder in a house cat. I am secretly a child of the woodland and forest. I still shower under water breaking over rocks. I see a thousand diamonds in the morning dew outside of our kitchen window. I can still imagine my husband embracing me like lions must mate, even if he has forgotten what he is doing when he embraces me in bed. He comes to me as though trying to remember whether this is a good or a bad habit, like the way he eats globs of cherry vanilla ice cream, wondering whether he should heave it up because he suddenly remembers its cholesterol count. My husband is one year older than I and he has just fallen victim to bulletins from the National Institutes of Health.

I can see only a few boats on the water. Sailing is for Saturdays and Sundays in Larchmont. The rest of the week is for good old-fashioned Puritan work, which includes the Protestant, Catholic, and Jewish populations who equally divide this village by the sea only thirty-five minutes from Grand Central Station. My husband complains of the train ride but I never believe him. I know he loves the company of the men on the train, that the best part of his day is the morning when he and his friends meet on the station platform and share a Penn Central seat for four and talk their way into Grand Central Station like priests mumbling their

4

vows over and over again. I don't know a man who isn't happier with other men than with his wife, at least from what I hear on the tennis courts in Larchmont and in that vulnerable institution, the Club, where the men isolate themselves as though exogamous rules toward wives are pasted on the grand mahogany bulletin board where the tides are listed.

My husband is the Executive Vice-President of the New York Family Health Plan Foundation, one of those great schemes to keep thousands of people healthy so that they will not cause enormous problems when they enter the nursing homes of the future.

You will have to excuse me. I may have been the one who ruined your child's life. For a brief period of my life I was a teacher. What teachers do lasts a lifetime. Everybody else in this world has only a limited influence on someone else's life. Teachers influence the mind for all of life even after we have forgotten what we have learned—and what we were taught to unlearn.

I didn't come to teaching from one of those rigid education schools that exist to send armies of teachers into the field to seek and destroy children. I studied at Smith where bright young ladies learn to keep their minds as taut as a chestnut mare. There is a time in our lives which begins when we are born, when the world comes to us in all of its glorious invention. When every moment of our lives is filled with an excitement we absorb with our bones. Sunsets. Trees. Leaves. Grass. Air. Sunlight. Faces. Bodies. Butterflies. Water. Each living thing with its own special smell. Music. The song of birds. The sudden leap of a cat. Clouds moving across the sky. Thunder. Rain. Night. Voices. Touch and feel. Can you imagine today what your feelings must have been when you first saw the world without the blinders of the world we now live in? That memory is lost.

I gave up teaching when I realized I was participating in the destruction of the dream of discovery. Discovery ends when a child enters a school. A new memory, built piece by piece by teachers, begins to replace the memory of the newborn child, until the child forgets all he has known and begins to remember only what he is taught to remember. The days of childhood are lost forever. This is known as childhood amnesia. It is the loss of our discovery of the natural world. I could no longer face the children who came into my class freshly scrubbed, bearing the marks of their mothers who were filled with fear that their children would lose the race. Never mind if all the children lost the race, if only their child won the race. The mothers never knew their children had already lost the race.

I became an assistant to a publisher on Madison Avenue who wore blue bow ties and shirts made in London, but who failed, unlike Henry Adams, to have his shirts returned to London for ironing. I left the publisher and in rapid succession found a series of jobs that always seem to be available to women in New York who don't know what else to do. When I found myself drifting toward Lexington Avenue and the crowds heading for Bloomingdale's as though Bloomingdale's was the temple of true salvation, I decided to try and write a novel.

The novel did not get written, but I never forgot the excitement of working on it. I think if I had dared then, I might have uncovered the childhood memory I had lost as has everyone else on earth. Now I am willing to dare. Not by writing that novel. Novels that uncover dreams are seldom read. We panic at the thought of coming face to face with ourselves. This is why the greatest novelists were clever enough to write their best novels about people who could never be our next-door neighbors. Flaubert tried with *Madame Bovary* and the French tried to suppress *Madame Bovary* and imprison Flaubert. The French reviewers hacked Flaubert to pieces, but the miracle is that Flaubert grew new limbs as quickly as they were hacked off. *Madame Bovary* outlived every one of her critics. I studied *Madame Bovary* at Smith and would never have known that French critics hacked Flaubert to pieces without my professor giving me that bit of historical information as a caution against deserting the teaching profession for novel writing.

It is 3:30 and I do not have to worry about dinner. In our house we have grown accustomed to barbecued chicken from the delicatessen during the summer months. For reasons that none of the young sociologists who write for *Commentary* magazine have tried to pierce with their eyeless gaze, charcoal broiling in the backyard has gone the way of the basement playroom. Americans who recently came out of the cellar have now come away from barbecue pits.

The Blue Jay is marvelous to handle. The boat responds to my lightest touch. The Blue Jay will be raced by my son during Larchmont Race Week. My husband wants Michael to win. The gold cup will runneth over for my husband if Michael wins. He will be able to buy drinks at the Club without the waiter asking his name.

I have another plan for my son. A plan that not even

Shakespeare dared to show to the Elizabethan audiences.

First let me tell you about my son. I was married when I was twenty-two. Michael is fifteen. If I am right Michael was conceived after my husband treated me to a meal at the Four Seasons and rushed me home to bed as though I was the dessert the waiter was slow in bringing. The check was sixty-seven dollars and I responded accordingly. The tragedy of sex is that it is not conceived as sex. It is revenge or reward. Mostly revenge. It is a game that I play as well as anyone else, if I am to grade myself by the ladies in white tennis dresses who walk into the Grand Union supermarket with their bottoms showing. I am breaking no great vow of secrecy if I tell you that women are much freer now in telling other women about their husbands, which used to be the way the ladies of the court in olden days passed their time. The unexpurgated *Arabian Nights* is much more revealing than Masters and Johnson, who after all are a business.

My son is fifteen. He is tall. He is handsome. He has the look of upper-middle-class children, the hopeful confidence that he will get a Porsche on graduating from high school. Some settle for an Audi. He has a flat stomach. A beautiful tan. He is a green belt in karate. His muscles are true ribbons of steel. Karate has given him the grace of a ballet dancer without the bland look of male dancers. Michael reads two books a week. His favorite author was F. Scott Fitzgerald until he read Steinbeck, but now he has returned to Fitzgerald because "Fitzgerald is more inventive, you feel what he is writing, Steinbeck just tells you what to see." That is a direct quote from Michael.

We have a big house even for Larchmont. The three of us don't need sixteen rooms but we bought our house when $100,000 houses were still selling for $65,000. I can see our house from the Blue Jay. It is white, with three columns, a slate roof. Michael has a room shaped like a Norman tower. He told me he was going up to his room to rest when I told him I was taking out the Blue Jay. It is the room where he has lived most of his life. It is twenty by twenty feet with big windows facing the Sound. From his bed Michael can see the boats on the water, the white sails, whose shape is one of the most beautiful sights on earth. The room is decorated like the interior of a yacht with bits and pieces of old sailing boats that we picked up in a junkyard store in Connecticut. There is a marvelous old brass compass set on top of a polished mahogany base and a beautiful ship's clock that rings its bells. A sea chest bound in iron, bearing the name of Captain Elmer Smith of New Bedford, is set at the foot of Michael's bed, holding paperback books. The walls are white and the two-hundred-year-old beams from a Vermont farmhouse have blended in nicely with the 1910 Larchmont summer cottage architecture. The walls are hung with primitive American sea paintings that Philip insists are worth a fortune today. Michael sails the Blue Jay with an eloquent confidence that Philip could never seem to bring to sailing.

I haven't yet spoken to Michael about his relationship with girls. I assume he has a primitive knowledge of girls; what other kind of knowledge is obtainable to him? I hope to change that.

I asked Philip if he spoke to Michael about girls. Philip said, "What is there to tell him? Kids today know everything." But do they? If parents don't know more than their limited experience, if the schools only teach what the teachers know, which is hopelessly primitive, then where are children to get their knowledge? TV or the R movies that treat sex like wrestling matches? Please excuse me if I don't believe that our children (c. 1976) have inherited a wild, wonderful, exalted view of sex that was supposed to be obtainable only in Parisian whorehouses. The American way is to view sex as a doomsday machine. Yet, there are moments in our lives when we seem to forget all of the lies that have been told us about sex. They come when we are as ready and ripe as young corn. When we seem to relive the time we first saw a tree, a buttercup, another human being. The time before our senses were drummed out of us by millions of TV commercials advertising cleanliness as the greatest virtue of modern life—the deodorization of our bodies as a triumph over nature. We mothers know it even if we try to conceal the fact, we know that our children can recognize us by our smell. Children delight in the smell of their own bodies and this delight, as we know, is forced out of them until it becomes a memory as lost as the excitement that preceded their birth. Michael said to me, "Did you know who I was when I was inside of you?"

The sea has the odor of freshness we have lost. I love the feel of my body after I have been on our thirty-one-foot *Sea Islander* for two or three days. My body never feels so soft, so clean. My skin is permitted to breathe, to come alive, to shine, after a five-day sail to Block Island. The wind off the Atlantic is soft unless the sea heaves and the skies grow dark. I have seen waves hurl over the bow of our *Sea Islander.* We have floundered in the Atlantic and it was God's guess as to whether we would come out alive. Our *Sea Islander* is weighted with one ton of ballast, but steamers have gone down off the coast of Block Island and for centuries boats have been hurled against the rocks of Mohegan's Bluff. The sea is no toy. Even Long Island Sound can be dangerous. Philip says I shouldn't take out the Blue Jay alone. But I am never alone on the water. I am alive on the water. There are two of me on the water. The old me that never gets sorted out and the me of the water that understands the changing sky, the wind, the color and play of the water, and all the danger signs.

There is more to the water. The sea is the mother of us all. We fling ourselves into the sea. We ride the waves. We love the surf. We offer our bodies to the surf. We delight in the tide that pulls us out into the ocean even when we are afraid of the tide. For centuries men have been the sailors. Few women if any have ever been captain of a boat. Men have known the sensual pull of the sea. It is men who have driven the boats into the sea, separating the sea as they would a woman's legs. It is at sea that men are most erotic, even Philip. He loves nothing better than to close the hatch on the *Sea Islander,* prop me up against the cushions that serve as a bed at the cabin table, bring my legs up to his shoulders, and enter me as he would a northwind.

When I am alone in the boat I am at the tiller, in full command. The design of all boats is masculine and feminine. It is nature in her most untroubled design. The male is easily seen in the long sweep of the boat, in the bow that enters the sea. The woman is easily seen in the hull of the boat.

I grow aroused in the boat, even as I look out for floating lobster pots. I am aroused from the moment I step into the boat off the Club launch. The pulling up of the sails, the tying of the ropes, the readiness to cast off, the first full free pull of the boat, the sudden, always lovely feel of the wind, the sails filling out, taking to the sky, the land pulling away, the sweep of water, my grip on the tiller, all tells me why I sail.

It is hard for me to describe myself. Women are always looking into mirrors and seeing what isn't on the face of the mirror. I don't know to what advantage it was for God to make each one of us look different. There is an ancient saying that tells us God made each person different because he didn't want any favorites. It is a nice legend but there are favorites and the favored of this world know who they are. The rest of us look into mirrors. I am five feet four inches tall. I have brown hair I wash myself and it hasn't been ruined by the beauty operators in Larchmont or the East 50s in New York. I love cottage cheese. I have kept my figure, or tennis has kept my figure, even though I am beginning to hate tennis because of the rush of people to play tennis who don't know how to swing a racket. Tennis has entered big money and that makes it the most respectable game now in America. Housewives are rushing to buy seventy-five-dollar tennis rackets. Books, tennis, music, ballet, movies, restaurants, all are judged by money. We have lost our respect for achievement. We have extinguished achievement under a flood of dollars. I am best described by the fact that I believe in my ideas because after a time we no longer see a person, except for a hopeful expectation that our friends will one day reveal themselves to us. Most people have a remarkable gift for telling us exactly what they are not.

I have only the credentials of a housewife, but I think I am on to something of extraordinary importance in the life of this planet, and for that reason I ask you to bear with me while I stumble through the preliminaries of introducing myself to you.

I am not one of those people who is impressed by credentials. I realize credentials have their place in the pecking order, but in the life and death of this planet credentials have no place. It is time for the natural reverberations of our minds to be felt. I don't mean the reverberations that come from hashish or LSD or any of the drugs that limit our knowledge to despair. I mean the reverberations that are sunk into our bones like radiation, that live in each of us like the carbon content in rocks and minerals, that go back into the time before we had any written or verbal knowledge, reverberations that are as much a part of us as our skin and bones, reverberations that have been silenced by centuries of laws and codes and regulations, the great taboos, the enforcing arm, those still lingering voices that tell us to do what is right or else the hounds of heaven will drive us into hell. Surely you have felt the reverberations.

Let me try and be more sure of what I am saying. Reverberations come over us in unguarded moments when we feel the universe ought to have a unity, a unity we may have felt in the days before the loss of our first childhood memory. Then we galloped down the corridors of time without fear, loving every minute of our lives, delighting in every sight and sound that was before our eyes and ears. In the daily life we have invented for ourselves we are filled with tension, fragments of experience, a list of no's from here to Sunday, sudden fears that shake our bodies, voices shouting at us to be ourselves even when we don't know what we are. The fear, tension, anxiety, doubt, brooding, all this dates from the loss of our first childhood memory and is calculated to keep us on the razor's edge. Yet from dawn to dusk, from the time we are taught a new memory, from that moment when we leave the childhood world of extraordinary sounds and dazzling invention, we long for a memory we have forgotten. We can never completely shut it out. The bits and glimpses of that memory fill us with a longing that we attribute to a love for God, or the search for some kind of unity in the universe that probably doesn't exist—and what if it does, what will that prove to us? That we share the same destiny as an atom of hydrogen, or the planet Venus?

At Smith I wrote a paper where I said artists and writers struggle to work their way out of the jaws of heaven. I wondered why artists struggle to tell people what they do not want to know. The greatest book is a hopeless cry of rage at being unable to know the past. The greatest painters spend their lives painting pictures trying desperately to reclaim their lost memory. Look at the late work of Calder, Miró, Picasso, the brooding pictures of Rembrandt which always escape joy. I wrote how all societies must make people work and forget freedom because men and women would rather loll like a cat and eat only the fruit that drops from a tree and embrace only within their own family.

People must be made to work and forget freedom. To make people work, the joy of discovery must be eliminated from the child's mind. The child must be given a new memory, a memory with a watch that ticks off the seconds, with a calendar, with books, alphabet, rules; a memory that slowly and without witness on our part wipes out our childhood past as a wave wipes out the pattern of children's feet on the beach. This new memory we call life. As long as we live we are confused by what we call life because at the back of our heads, deep in some part of our bodies that escapes even the meanest X rays, is a part of us that never dies —the past that is the first memory of life in this world.

When did I first feel these reverberations, these feelings that boom out of the universe like the rays from the sun? At the birth of Michael I saw how he enjoyed his existence and then, little by little, I saw that joy slip away from him until he became like all other children. I saw that there is something in this life called childhood amnesia. I knew what it was when I saw Michael, no longer an infant, look up every so often as though he were trying to see himself in a mirror, to remember who he was. Freud was astonished to learn his patients could not recall their earliest childhood days, not the simplest memories, the most carefree days. Freud saw adults left with half-remembered fragments, recalling experiences of experiences they were taught to remember, but nothing of their earliest childhood days when they had a free memory.

Marcel Proust tried to recall his memory, but he only succeeded in making it more elusive. His gift to us was to tell us that we cannot recall the memory taken from us. The memory we have as adults is just a grocery shopping list of dates and anniversaries, a handful of fragments which seem like everyone else's experiences.

The reverberations we feel are the forgotten memories of a childhood that is beyond recall, that I saw Michael trying to recall. How can I tell you what it was like for me to first eat an orange, see a pool of water, watch a caterpillar, touch a leaf, touch my mother, feel my father, see the sun. All this is forgotten. What I now remember is that it is important for me to make breakfast, important to know the schedule of trains from Larchmont into New York City. At funerals we remember life. This is because we all know that something important to us died early in all of our lives. We constantly long for the past but it is a false past, since it is beyond recall. The past escaped Proust; the past was never fully available to Freud. The past is what I now want Michael to understand in a way that was never possible for me, because no one in my family dared.

So here I am on a Blue Jay off the shore of Larchmont, a village of seven thousand on the Westchester coast, getting great pleasure out of sailing my Blue Jay but more pleasure out of talking to you, feeling the Blue Jay make its way through the water into the mother of us all, the sea, which I love as though it were my daughter. The Blue Jay is racing the clouds, the threat of thunder clouds as far away as Glen Cove. I would almost like to be caught in a sudden squall, to feel the wind tearing at the sails, trying to rip apart the mast, and race the squall to the shore, heeling over so that I am almost part of the sea. The sea is alive with the past and has no lost memories.

I am not Proust, but I may once have been more successful than Proust. I was out on the Sound, a day like today, great billowing clouds, a stiff breeze, high tide, the water soaking up the blue from the sky, the white houses on the shore looking like a village in Greece, the Larchmont shore bursting with green after a two-day rainfall. I found myself trembling with excitement, a tingling I couldn't explain. I looked up at the clouds and found myself looking into a cloud shaped like an ice cream cone. I shouted, "Look, there's an ice cream cone, look at the cloud, it's an ice cream cone, there's an ice cream cone!" There was nothing more exciting in the universe to see. The cloud engulfed me. I felt myself lifted into the cloud. The cloud was a memory stretching back to 1939. I was licking something I didn't have the words to describe. Later I learned it was ice cream, made by Bassett's in Philadelphia. I was one year old. When we are one year old we do not have words yet to describe our experiences, that is one of the reasons why we can't remember a first ice cream or the first touch of water. In 1939 I had no words to describe the taste of ice cream. Eating ice cream was one of the million experiences seeking my attention.

I detest it when children enter school and have that early memory taken from them as though it were a leper that must be driven into isolation. Let a little of that memory linger. But there is too much freedom in that memory. The youth in the 1960s tried to reclaim that memory but they were

17

wiped out as though they were an invading army of barbarians. They were fed drugs to stop the search for their memory. If you have a creative child now you will understand why the public schools are forced to destroy your child. Teachers detest creative children. They love the straight A's. The creative child is abandoned. There are few teachers in the land who know how to work with a creative child. What happens to the children who are not creative, who are not straight A's? They become you and me, longing for a past we will never be able to recognize.

Think back, young mothers. A generation ago children entered school at the age of six or seven. The very rich sent their children to day schools at the age of three or four, or had tutors for them. Today children are in day schools at the age of two. The children of today have half the childhood they had a generation ago. In the same way the Chinese send their children to school at the age of two and even one year of age, to wipe out their childhood memory. The Chinese and the Russians know that children without a childhood memory have no past that tells them they were once free.

This is what an afternoon of sailing on the Sound does for me: questions that remain submerged at breakfast float to the surface.

But this is no ordinary afternoon. I am taking the Blue Jay in to shore now. I will anchor the Blue Jay at the Club. I will have a gin and tonic before getting into my blue Mercedes for the three-minute drive to our white sixteen-room house. In the Blue Jay, on the Sound, I utter every thought I know Philip wouldn't listen to as he groans about living on two thousand calories a day, nearly four times as many calories as the rest of the world lives on. Philip is hopelessly resigned to survival. He has set his sights, as they used to say in Ohio, on living past seventy, which he would consider a triumph over his diet.

I have set my sights on my son Michael. He must not enter the new world of the twenty-first century with the bad habits of all the centuries that preceded him. I am not prepared to watch Michael drift into his twenties and thirties wondering where life has gone, wondering why no woman is capable of giving him an exquisite delight that no man can define, yet all seem to yearn for, as Philip does when he leaves our bed as though denied a piece of candy.

I don't want Michael to be forever bewildered by women. I don't want him wondering where his life has gone, feeling himself this double being that can look in on himself without knowing himself, drifting like a sluggish tide into boredom, thrusting himself into women as if trying to find a golden peacock. I am responsible for Michael being on this earth. I taught him to eat, to sit on the toilet, to be brave about walking. I could have denied him existence by telling Philip I had a headache.

I know what I must do. I think it is what every woman would do, and what women have done without giving it as much thought as I have. But then I have had my habits shaped by Philadelphia, Shaker Heights, Park Avenue, private schools in the East 60s, and finally Smith College which taught me how much there is to unlearn. I will sail the Blue Jay to shore. I will have my gin and tonic. I will pull into our driveway. I will go up to the third floor where Michael is sleeping. I will get into bed with Michael. I will see whether the world comes tumbling down. Yes, yes, yes, I think we long for our forgotten childhood with a desire that we have no words for. I think we long with more intensity than we ever dare show to physically enter the bodies of our parents, to sleep with them, to feel the everlasting comfort that was so rudely interrupted by life. A comfort denounced in every corner of the world. A comfort denied by laws, sanctions, death, stoning, poison, fire. Yet few among us ask why such a comfort should be so violently denied. We spend our lives in hopeless confusion trying to find a moment of comfort. It is here in my body. It haunts every dream I have. I won't let it haunt me any longer. Or my son.

Michael

I wish I had started keeping a diary from the day I first learned to write. Words seem to be the only thing that tells us we are alive. Even our voices are words. The deaf don't speak but they live on words. They learn to read with their hands. Probably they have an inner voice that never reaches us. My cousin Richard is deaf and I can tell by his eyes that he knows the words he cannot speak. I know when my mother and my father are saying words they don't speak. But that isn't too exceptional. It is a mystery to me why we spend so much time hiding ourselves from one another. When I read Charles Dickens he makes it so easy for you to know all the hundreds of characters who run through his books. It isn't that way in life. My mother and my father sometimes stare at me in awe the way they would at a plant wondering how I will bloom, if I will bloom at all. It is as though I am something planted in the soil that needs to be watered every other day and one day I will be like the plant on the package of seeds.

I do not believe that we are supposed to wait to become what we are. I think it is the idea of waiting that is driving the kids I know crazy. David tells me he wants to be free now. The idiot. None of us is free if you read Euripides. Every book that I read tells me that I am not free. Poor Thoreau. He lived in a hut by a pond and talked to the birds and wanted to follow a bird to its resting place, thinking the bird would lead him out of the woods. This is the madness we are made of. And Thoreau is one of our geniuses, one of the first men in this country to take time to think. The rest of the men were too busy working, exploring, traveling West, building railroads, discovering coal, oil, gas, steam, the dynamo, electricity, cities, silver, gold, factories, and finding out that men were cheaper than animals.

My social science teacher who managed to survive the Vietnam war told us that all history is shit. "When I got out of that stinking war I went back and read every newspaper in New Rochelle going back to 1967 and not a single edition ever told me what that war was like." I liked him for saying that. The kids in the class started clapping. It was a great glorious moment. All my other teachers act as if they are going to be called before a tribunal that will sentence them to death if they dare to smile or say something that will make them sound human.

I sometimes get the eerie feeling that we are the first generation in the history of the world being trained not to be human. Hitler did it with his generation for a few short years, and he succeeded. I wonder if he would have succeeded with me. Could somebody make me inhuman? Could I kill on command? Smash a baby against a brick wall? Kill old people? Press the trigger on a machine gun and shoot down a row of people like dominoes? No, Hitler could not do that to me. I suppose I could become another inhuman kind of person. I could work for government in a bureaucracy and sentence people to food stamps for the rest of their lives. I could be like my Uncle Robert and deny people their applications for loans to buy a house. Is it true that 80 percent of the American people who now want to own a home can't afford to buy a home? My father tells me we are witnessing the liquidation of the middle class. There will be the rich and other people, he says at dinner. He means for me to be rich. That means I will have to be inhuman to the others. I think in the world to come we will not bother to psychologically destroy people as Orwell tells us. I think we will bring unwanted people to special elimination arenas and annihilate them in a great burst of flame.

This is not so farfetched. At dinner Friday night, Dr. Fields and my father were talking about welfare. Dr. Fields said there is a simple solution. This is what he said: "Those people are useless. They will never work. No jobs will ever exist for them. They are useless, superfluous people. The way to solve the welfare problem is to shoot all of the people on welfare. Then you won't have a problem. I do not believe in keeping alive people who are useless and a drain." Dr. Fields is a medical doctor. He spoke in all seriousness. As he spoke you could see people driven out of their homes and shot in Yankee Stadium with city sanitation dump trucks carrying the bodies away to be used as fuel for the steam plants. I thought my father would hit him in the mouth. But my father is polite to the extreme or else scared shitless of Dr. Fields or anyone else when it comes to opposing an opinion. My mother said, "You are full of shit, Don." Dr. Fields said, "Then *you* feed the pigs on welfare." My mother said, "From your table." If it wasn't for the fact that I know my mother has been fucked by Dr. Fields I would have thought they were arguing. Dr. Fields is one of our oldest friends. I don't know if my father knows or doesn't know or pretends not to know, but in any case it doesn't seem to make any great difference in our house. Dr. Fields fucked my mother before she married my father. I know that from some letters I read in the attic that may actually have been left there by mother for me to read. Whether my mother still fucks Dr. Fields is not a piece of knowledge I am privy to.

I see no purpose now in keeping a diary. I have been reading the diary of Kafka and all he does is piss and moan and say he would like to die to be reborn. Reborn to what? Like every kid in Larchmont who wants to be different. Different from what, to what, I ask. I hate the whole nostalgia bit. Mark's parents have a house on Pryor Lane where every house costs more than $150,000. Their house is crazy. When you walk into the living room all you see are Coca-Cola signs. There is a Coca-Cola mirror, a Coca-Cola lamp, a Coca-Cola scale, pictures, posters, bottles, flags. Nobody on earth can tell me that a Coca-Cola sign from 1910 is anything but a piece of crap. It was made as crap, it was crap in 1910, 1920, 1930, 1970, and now in the Feldman living room. I asked Mark what he thinks of all the shit. He said to me, "They don't fuck anymore so let them enjoy their toys. I think my father plays with the old cars and then goes into the bedroom to whack off. He's always making speeches that he thinks are in fun, of how whacking off is better than fucking. He's not joking." Or take Jimmy's house. His father boasts that their living room is furnished with the crap that people have thrown out on the curb in Larchmont. He goes out every night in his $18,000 Mercedes and cruises Larchmont looking for shit on the curb. He has three broken chairs in the living room that wouldn't bring ten dollars at a tag sale. He has a couch that he dragged into the house with Jimmy screaming, "Throw this piece of shit away, Dad." It's not that Jimmy's father can't afford a Sloane sofa for fifteen hundred dollars. I think it is because his father cannot afford to be without some kind of dream, some kind of personal victory other than pulling out other people's teeth. How can anybody be different in a world that is the same every day? Does wearing a pair of ripped-up old jeans make you different when every other kid is wearing ripped-up old jeans? Does it make you different when your tits bob as you walk without a brassiere when every girl and woman on this earth has two tits and why it continues to be a source of mystery is beyond my small mind to comprehend. Was Carl different when he walked out of his $190,000 house with no money in his pocket, no shoes, no jacket, his hair down to his waist, and disappeared into the woods near Larchmont for five days while his parents sat by the telephone as though he had been kidnapped by Al Capone. He never told any of us what he did for five days in Saxon Woods, but it couldn't have been much except to be cold and hungry, and maybe that isn't such a bad feeling if you are fed more than you can eat every day of your life.

A diary would have given me a record of my life. I would have known what I felt like ten years ago, five years ago. It wouldn't have to be jerked out of me, the way Seth describes his sessions with his psychiatrist on East 83rd Street. "I invent half of the crap for him. I can't remember anything. What's there to remember? The son of a bitch doesn't listen. He plays with his balls and stares at the clock as though it were a slot machine. I have no memory. Fuck memories. What good are they? It's the future that counts. I can't stand those fucking books where they tell you everything. How the guy opened a door, closed a door, blew his nose, took his cock out to fuck, ate a ham and cheese sandwich, drank a whiskey, sucked a cunt, stepped into his car or jumped out of a window. I bullshit that horny doctor. He doesn't give a shit about me. I hear he is seeing two different psychiatrists for his own troubles. He sometimes starts to doze off. That's when I invent a horny story like getting a thrill out of licking armpits or wanting to smell my mother's underwear and he writes the gibberish in a pad on his desk. I wonder if my seeing that horny bastard will keep me from getting an automobile license." Seth tells me he is going to Harvard and then the Harvard School of Business Administration because that is where it's going to be at and the only fun left in this world will be telling other people what to do and knowing the poor fuckers can't do a thing about it. Seth says we will all be in a trap and his freedom will be keeping other people from getting their freedom. "I need Harvard to be free, not some creepy analyst who scratches his balls." Why do we long for freedom when we haven't the faintest notion of what freedom is, except that my father tells me it's easier to be free with money than without money.

The Blue Jay is freedom. I have to give my parents credit for buying the Blue Jay when I was young enough to sail naturally and not be puzzled by all the ropes and sails and how it sailed. I like being on the water. I don't like the Club. But I don't have to like the Club to be on the water. The Club is a convenience. For most of the people the Club is life. It is like a monument with a long flight of steps and on top of the steps is the Club and that is life. Some women spend ten hours a day at the Club. They go from tennis to swimming to sailing to drinking and talking. Their parents belonged to the Club, they belong to the Club, their children belong to the Club. Their children wear blue blazer jackets, gray slacks, white shirts, and they stand at attention at the flagpole and wear the same faces as their parents, the unblinking satisfaction of the good life. But if the life is so good why are the Bloody Marys so much better than lemonade and why do they get drunk on Friday night, on Saturday night, and talk to one another in a garbled drunken language where it takes two minutes for a simple sentence to come out and the women look like they are going to run down into the water and cut their throats with the steak knives.

We are members only for the two boats we dock. The rest of the Club I ignore. I have never eaten at the buffet table because it does not look like a place to break bread but to lose your marbles. The boating rooms of the Club are splendid—that is the correct word—with oil paintings of former commodores and great ships, brass and mahogany, teak, stainless steel, the past forever present. Those stalwart men in the oil paintings did know how to sail ships. They sailed the Atlantic in sleek sailing ships and raced in boats faster than a whale. They fought storms in the North Atlantic and in the fog around Block Island. In the 1900s they docked at the Club in two-hundred-foot yachts and sailed the Sound like Arabian kings, only they were more powerful. Morgan came, and the Vanderbilts, and the sea was a carpet for them. The Club is not that elegant today. It is for boozing and boating. Everybody seems to have a boat today. It is silly to live in Larchmont without a boat. You will never know Larchmont unless you sail. But the grandeur of the Club has been cut down to the size of a Blue Jay.

I will win the Blue Jay race. I know my boat. It is the fastest Blue Jay on the Sound. I have raced it since I was ten years old. I talk to the boat. The boat listens to me. It responds to my touch and tells me when danger is coming. My Blue Jay has never capsized. It would be unthinkable, like our house tumbling down. I love it on the water. The smartest thing my father and mother ever did was to buy the Blue Jay. The boat has given me the sun and the sky and the water. I hear distant bells. I see the swinging light of a beacon. I see the buoys popping out of the water. I know the exact angle that a boat will cross my path. I have developed a fine sense of loathing for powerboats that roar around in the Sound like motorcycles. I move with winds as ancient as the beginning of the world. I am never alone. I know some of my friends are alone in the midst of rock sound coming from sixteen speakers. The sound of the sea gulls doesn't need a KLH amplifier.

I don't like to race to win. I race because that is the way I know my boat and I are pulling together, telling each other what we have learned on the water. I am fascinated by water. The oceans sit at our shores like they will drown us at any moment. A slight lifting of the table of water and the tides will sweep over the world. But the oceans are good to us and they remain patiently at the shoreline. We have nothing to fear from the oceans. I have never been out in the boat in a storm that frightened me.

A million things frighten me on shore. I do not like pills. I have seen too many pills swallowed in this house and other houses. I do not like automobiles. They make too much noise and cause too much pollution. They have become dangerous weapons. I stopped reading the daily newspaper because it always has nothing to say in a world where there seems to be a need to explain every action. I hate television. I have stopped watching the evening news because I know the evening news is nothing more than a trap to get me to accept violence, murder, terror, as the daily order of things. I wonder if the newscasters know how evil they are in preparing this generation to be murderers. I hate the atomic bomb. The atomic bomb won an instant victory over my generation. The bomb created a new world in which everything is expendable. The bomb wiped out the value of things. The bomb took away the timelessness of living. I do not know what to say to the bomb. I do not know if

Thoreau would have anything to say to the bomb. The bomb sits above us. The bomb will not go away. We must learn to live with it like those people who live on the slope of a slumbering volcano or those people who always rebuild their homes where a flood has torn away their houses.

I enjoy my summer naps. My room is cool. There is always a breeze from the Sound. Sometimes the sky lights up with brilliant blues. But the dazzling sunsets seem to have vanished. The sky has to be filled with clouds of dust for brilliant sunsets. My room looks like a boat. I laid out my own room. It started with the compass I had my father buy me at the United House Wrecking Company in Stamford. Later we found hatch covers that we made into tables. Lights from old ships. Oars, oiled fishing hats, paintings of old sailing boats, a starter cannon, a map of the world printed in 1727.

The Larchmont Race Week starts tomorrow. The real estate agents like to say that Larchmont Race Week is famous all over the world. I think they exaggerate. Larchmont Race Week used to be famous when the two-hundred-foot yachts would tie up in the harbor. The rich from all over the world would sit on deck and watch the Japanese lanterns swaying on shore while they tried to get along with five servants for every guest. I love the old paintings with the men in their white sailing caps and blue jackets bending over the Victorian ladies in their long gowns looking as sexy in their deck chairs as anything you can see in *Playboy.* The rich in those days looked rich. Not like the rich in Larchmont today. But Larchmont is a rich town, except for the families who are coming in from the Bronx and Manhattan who have borrowed every penny they could from insurance policies, relatives, pension funds, credit unions, to make a deposit on a $76,000 house that would be worth $32,000 in Cleveland, Ohio. Larchmont thinks it is in a no-fire zone. A DMZ. But the day will come when crime won't stop at the border of the northern Bronx and the kids who kill in the West Bronx and South Bronx will cross into Pelham, New Rochelle, Larchmont, and the ladies in white will be afraid to go out of their house to play tennis. Nobody is fooling anybody if they think and believe Larchmont is in a no-fire zone just because the rich choose to live here. When the rich decide to leave and race their boats in Greenwich or farther up the Sound, then the schoolteachers who bought $76,000 houses will find themselves sitting up nights in their living room with a shotgun to protect their deposit.

Right now Larchmont is all trees and shaded roads leading to the Sound. And white cottages built in 1910 for Broadway actresses who wanted to screw with a cool breeze blowing through the bedroom. There is a story that John Barrymore went down on Carole Lombard in Larchmont, but if Barrymore didn't then somebody else did. Larchmont is full of legends. It doesn't make any difference whether they are true or not, the legends are believed because it keeps real estate values up.

My father wants me to win the race Sunday. My mother couldn't care less. We both know that sailing is more than winning a race. My father is a man I would like to know a little better one day. He seems confused by me. At times he looks at me as though he bought the wrong shirt size at Brooks Brothers. I don't think he ever expected to have a son. He wasn't prepared for me. I am a real living person that he brought into the world and I wouldn't exist without him, and I think he can't associate the miracle of my birth with what he does every day, which seems to be to fight with my mother at breakfast and then ride the train into New York, and then ride the train at 5:15 back to Larchmont and start to fight again with my mother, and then sulk in the sun room. And when it seems like it is time to go to sleep, he goes to sleep, and then he wakes up to do the same thing again, except on Friday he likes to eat out at a Chinese restaurant where he seems to be happy when he is chewing on barbecued spareribs. But he bought me the Blue Jay. That was an inspired act. I am not putting down my father. He has to work hard to support this house and what would he do if he didn't work. I think my father is unhappy that he didn't become a doctor or a lawyer or some kind of a professional with a title. He likes to say they are the happiest idiots in America. I see it at Mamaroneck High School. The teachers with a doctorate degree don't feel like ordinary teachers, they walk like politicians, and they expect flags to be waving in their path. My father says I should go to Harvard and get a B.A., an M.B.A., and a Ph.D. because in the new world around the corner credentials will be worn on your lapel the way identification cards are worn at the Pentagon, and you will be either in or out. "The new world will have no place for the marginal man like me," my father says almost weekly when we go to the Chinese restaurant and he feels expansive. "The new world will have kings and coolies, the ins and the outs; perception, creativity, understanding, compassion will all be shit words, nothing will count but your credentials, like in ancient China, when men with the degrees ruled, and the rest of the Chinese took orders. I never got my full credentials at Harvard even though I understood the process then. I just hope I can hang on long enough before the trapdoor is closed. The new world is going to be brutal but at least the people with credentials will have some of the goodies. That, Michael, is the extent of my knowledge about the future. Get your degrees, get your credentials." The kids I know in Larchmont are generous to their parents. They don't put their parents down. They understand the hassle their parents are in and they admire the courage their parents show in getting out of bed every morning and doing what they do, even if they don't fly test planes to the moon. Not everybody has a Carole Lombard to nuzzle in Larchmont.

My mother is the mystery of our family. Sometimes I see a blue flame coming from her eyes. My mother has no profession. Once she was a teacher but she says she hated teaching. She worked for a publisher but it was just answering the phone and doing some typing and not reading the first draft of a novel from Fitzgerald. I don't know how she feels about my father. She seems to accept him, like you accept a dog in the house without asking how the dog feels, if the dog would rather run free in the Larchmont conservation area instead of squatting in the kitchen and eating Purina Dog Chow. My mother often comes into my room wearing her bra and panties. My father yells at her for doing it. She says it is just like wearing a bikini. "The bikini even shows more." No, it doesn't. In the bra I can see my mother's nipples and I see them pop out and I know she is showing off her body to me. I can feel myself getting hard when she bends over and I can see her breasts. My mother's breasts look full, swaying. They seem to dance in front of my eyes. I know I sucked on them when I was young, but that was a long time ago and I have no memory of it except when my mother tells me how I used to bite and how much I preferred her milk to Dairylea. My mother has a great figure. She has a narrow waist and swelling hips and high breasts and her behind doesn't drop.

I heard a knock on my door and turned to see my mother.

Philip

From a window seat on the 3:40 afternoon train to Larchmont I stare at my fellow passengers with awe. They are real live people, ladies with elegant purple shopping bags from Bergdorf Goodman, ladies with shopping bags from Bloomingdale's, students with canvas bags slung over their shoulders, in jeans, as though Westchester County was a suburb of Montana. I am more used to the 5:15 evening train and the men who sit down in the plastic Penn Central seats as though they will never rise up again. Men who bury themselves in the only evening newspaper left in New York, the New York *Post,* dumbly reading the news as though each page carries their obituary. Most of the men fall asleep, waking up suddenly as the train pulls into the station, startled and dazed to go back to the business of living again, negotiating the trip home as though it were a game one has to practice endlessly before one gets it right.

I decided to flee New York this afternoon, to leave

my office early, without disturbing my secretary who was buried in a Gothic novel that seemed a thousand pages long, to abandon New York before the Friday gloom settled on the city. With the 3:40 train there would be time to take out the *Sea Islander* or the Blue Jay, to talk to Michael about the Blue Jay race on Sunday, or just to forget that the week begins again with Monday.

How easily civilizations come to an end. Architects are the first to forecast the ruins. In the dazzling mid-afternoon sunlight the Avenue of the Americas looked older than Stonehenge. The vast buildings rose straight up from the sidewalk of old Sixth Avenue as though they were built by a race of giant children playing with Lego blocks. It was not an inspiring sight to see your tomb rising all around you. The lobby of my building in the 50s has slabs of travertine marble wrapped around the elevator doors, the walls, the ceiling, floors, the architect inspired by a mausoleum. My father's biggest thrill was to stand in City Hall Park and stare at the old Woolworth Building and wonder at the race of men who had built it, just as Henry Adams wondered about the men who built the Gothic cathedrals. The slabs of fifty-story buildings on Sixth Avenue looked as though they would topple if I shoved out my hand and gave them a push, and for an inspired second I saw the buildings toppling like a row of dominoes, which was just about the fate they deserved.

Yet New York has always had a grandeur when the sun is shining and the filth in the air is momentarily swept aside by the breezes identified as coming from

Canada by TV weather forecasters who seem mad. Yesterday, Thursday, the soot and sulphur in the air, the automobile fumes, the exhaust from ten thousand buses charging up Madison Avenue, had settled over New York like a medieval plague and I thought I would have to crawl the last hundred yards to Grand Central.

Today the air was crisp and New York felt like a seafaring town. Who would dare believe the Atlantic Ocean was only a fifteen-minute subway ride away from Grand Central Station? For her birthday I took Elaine to dinner on the 107th floor of the World Trade Center building to see the Atlantic, and I thought how much my father would have liked the view which almost showed the world was round. I will never forget the Staten Island ferry rides I took with my father and his excitement when the skyline of New York came together like a giant church organ. "It is the greatest view in the world outside of the sun and the moon," my father said. Michael will probably never forget the sight of the tall ships that swept into New York harbor on July 4, 1976, the towering masts forming a triumphant cavalcade of the past. "You won't see anything like this anymore in Larchmont harbor," Michael said. Michael will win the Blue Jay race on Sunday.

I liked walking up Sixth Avenue at three in the afternoon, an hour when I am usually deep in dictation, sending memos to Washington, trying to reassure the medical profession that it will not lose holy ground if it agrees to support a health program that would eliminate the disease of doctor bills.

I liked the freedom of leaving my office early, a freedom I rarely permit myself because like most men I feel the world would crumble if I left before five. It was the freedom of a schoolboy cutting class, that marvelous elegiac sense I sometimes get when I leave the King Cole bar in the St. Regis Hotel at three in the afternoon after a long elegant lunch, brought to a fine edge by two martinis that turn everything in sight on Fifth Avenue into a mellow Vermont barn, weathered trees, a cool pond, with people ready to share with me their deepest confidences, all of it arousing in me a healthy sensuality that I suspect only shepherds still possess.

I walked past the 42nd Street Public Library remembering the astonishment in Michael's voice when he told me that his English teacher at Mamaroneck High informed the class that the 42nd Street Library had bookshelves under Bryant Park that went down thirty-seven floors. "Thirty-seven stories of books, all underground, it sounds like something you would expect at the end of the world," Michael said. Later it turned out the bookshelves only went down eight floors.

I walked past the old Automat opposite Grand Central Station where my father used to take me for lunch because I liked to shove nickels into the slots for cherry pie or a hot bowl of macaroni and cheese.

I crossed 42nd Street and walked into Grand Central Station like a visitor from another planet. It was not my time of day to be in Grand Central. The big round clock read 3:20. A hundred thousand men and women were still locked in their offices. They would not descend on Grand Central Station until five, their bodies pouring into the station like a river of concrete. Now the station was peopled with Westchester and

Connecticut housewives, carefully brushing back stray hair, carrying Louis Vuitton bags like banners. It looked like a pinball machine out of control, the lights blinking, the balls spinning, the only place to go was into the slots where the trains waited.

I found a seat on the 3:40 Larchmont train next to a lady who looked at me like I was a piece of furniture. Slowly, surely, even though it was the 3:40 train and not my usual 5:15 train, just as the train began to pull into the tunnel, I fell into that world between sleeping and dreaming, where night after night, year after year, I try to support the fiction that I am a husband, a father, a lover, a wage earner, a sailor, a homeowner, somewhat in control of my life, even though Elaine has the exquisite skill of making me feel that there are parts of my life that remain as remote to me as the dreams of our cat Jennie.

I like staring out of the train window even if there is nothing to see. The landscape is a blur and so are the people who live in the landscape, and I can rest until I reach my destination where my own life begins.

I am the man nobody knows. I am the man nobody knows. It was the first line that came to me for a speech I had to make in August. But no one listens to speeches anymore at the Hilton banquets. As soon as the ice cream cake with the strawberry sauce is devoured the guests flee toward the exits as though an army of muggers waits to murder all stragglers. Elaine thinks I love the ride into the city every morning, sitting and talking with Marty, Howie, O'Connell, Bates, mocking the *New York Times,* looking seriously at the front page of the *Wall Street Journal,* the talk politely orgiastic, with about as much lechery in all of us as a Mark Cross briefcase. I hate the train. I hate the sight of the men huddled over their cups of coffee, chewing on corn muffins, I hate the smoky waiting room, I hate the taxi drivers who all look like swindlers. I hate Grand Central Station which has sold itself cheaply to the Off-Track Betting Corporation, the OTB betting windows where the bettors line up like sheep at 9 A.M. to be slaughtered day in and day out. Nobody wins when everyone expects to lose.

I am the man nobody knows. Elaine, I am the husband you don't know. You aren't a wife to me. A wife should be like a mountain. A redwood tree. You should pick me up like the swells in the Atlantic. You should be the sun and my morning star. You should go down on me with the grace and beauty of a Japanese princess. You should be to me like the lighthouse on Block Island on Mohegan's Bluff, visible thirty-one miles out at sea. I need a lighthouse.

Elaine, why don't we sail the *Sea Islander* to the Caribbean? Bob Owens sailed to the Caribbean in his twenty-eight-foot boat. Owens was in heaven. "It's a different world, the stars as big as tennis balls." Yet when Owens came back from the Caribbean his wife swallowed exactly thirty-seven Thorazine pills, a pill for every year she lived.

When I get off the train I will tell Elaine that we will sell the house and move to California and buy a house on top of a mountain facing the Pacific Ocean. A health plan in San Francisco offered me the presidency at $100,000 a year. We could live on $100,000 in San Francisco. Elaine thinks I live to walk into the Club and order a Dewar's on the rocks. Fuck the Club.

I've never known who the Club belongs to. Everyone I know lives on the fringes of the Club, dues payers. I am tired of paying dues.

Elaine, I am not in a panic because I will soon be forty. I am not in a panic. I am calm and cool. I don't take a single tranquilizer. I don't drink to excess. I am only six pounds overweight. I can still jog three miles a night, down Beach Avenue, over to Fountain Square, around to Larchmont Avenue, down to the Post Road, over to Stuyvesant Avenue, past the Gothic windows, into Beach Avenue again, Manor Park, always chasing the moon, always baying like a werewolf, the villagers chasing me with pitchforks. They will hang my body up in the village square and spit on me until the full moon comes out, and only then will the werewolf in me be destroyed and a peaceful expression take over my face for eternity. Elaine, I want you to know that I am going to burn our house to the ground and walk away from the smoldering ashes. I won't let the volunteer Larchmont firemen put out the fire. We will take the insurance money and live in a camper in the Rocky Mountains. I hate the train, Elaine, you must believe that I hate the train and that I really want to live in a camper in the Rocky Mountains and eat Swedish pancakes for breakfast and fuck the cholesterol if I can have four happy years before I die forever.

Elaine, why don't we buy a house on Block Island and live like those pensioners who struggle through the sand to sit on the beach and watch the Atlantic? We will visit Block Island in November to see how strong the winds blow and if we can walk in the sand. I hear the wind cuts across the island and if you have a heart condition you can't walk into the wind. If you have arthritis you can't take the dampness from the ocean. Where will we live, Elaine? Where can we find a rock? We must flee Larchmont. Larchmont is a grave. The high-school-girl clerks in the Grand Union never say thank you to me when they ring up a seventy-five-dollar bill. They look at me like I am a ghost. Once, just once, I want one of them to smile at me and bend down so that I can see her breasts. Do you know what I want for my fortieth birthday, Elaine? A seventeen-year-old Larchmont girl with blond hair down to her waist who will tell me all the secrets she hides behind her polite smile. I want, I want, I want. The pity is that I don't know what I want, which is the oldest game I know how to play.

Elaine, why did the astronauts leave the moon? They could have been a symbol of escape for us. Even if one astronaut had died on the moon we would know that his human body was on the moon. I will bet my bottom dollar that the people in Zermatt want to flee to New York. Where can you flee from Larchmont? Nowhere else do people look as though the good things of this world are left on their doorstep every morning. I will not learn to play tennis. I will sail the *Sea Islander* into the North Atlantic and charge into an iceberg. All hands on deck. All hands on deck. Elaine, lay your magic hands on me. I am the man nobody knows. I am the captain and the only passenger. I am sailing into the twenty-first century unprepared for its wonders. I am always surprised at myself when I carefully screw in a fuse properly and the lights go on in the house.

My job is to keep doctors happy, rich, expansive, to remind them that they have the highest incomes in the nation, the best pensions, the longest holidays, the greatest freedom to treat their patients without being called to account. I honor them at yearly meetings for their dedication, devotion, and compassion to patients whose death certificates they sign like a Diner's Club card. Today at lunch I had iced coffee, a hamburger, apple pie and cherry vanilla ice cream, and I will survive my cholesterol. Elaine, let us flee New York. I want my marriage to be intact. I want my son to be intact. I want my life to be intact. I do not want to fly apart like a jet exploding in midair. I am sick of this train. I am sick of French restaurants. I am sick of orange juice and toasted English muffins. I want to grow old like those Greek men who live in white-walled villages. I want Michael to love me when I am eighty. I want to take long walks in the park and pick up runaway rubber balls for little children. Sometimes, Elaine, sometimes when we are in bed together, I look at you sleeping and I admire you for lying down next to me unafraid (which is what marriage is) and I think of the great miracle that brought us together. No one should be alone in this world. Every person in a mental hospital should be linked up with another person. The aged should be given a new partner if one should die. Everyone in this world should have someone to talk to who will listen, someone who will be there to watch him when he is ill and to say good-bye when he dies, and to weep. I think marriage is the rediscovery of our childhood. This is probably why my marriage persists. This is what the critics of marriage don't understand. The closer marriage gets to childhood, the more real the marriage becomes, because only children know how to be real. What I am saying is this, Elaine. If anything ever bothers you, if you feel troubled, if you want to shout it out and scream it at me, don't hold back because I won't know how to start all over again. I want our marriage to last. No suicides like Arnold Berg beating his steel tennis racquet against his office window, smashing the window until he made a hole big enough to jump through. The *New York Times* devoted a full page to the story, wondering how Berg with five hundred million in holdings could commit suicide. The *Times* never wonders why a man making twenty thousand a year commits suicide.

I will soon be home. I will swim. I will take the Blue Jay out with Michael. I will not jump from my forty-first-floor office window. I don't want anything to disturb Michael for the race on Sunday. Michael needs a victory. How strange to have a son who you feel still can't read you as clearly as he can the menu at the Larchmont Diner. This is not the way the animal kingdom sends its young into the world. There is not a kitten alive who does not know how to live. Where do we learn the nonsense we believe? Why do we have to spend our lives unlearning what we know? Elaine, maybe you are right when you talk about childhood amnesia, but you have never been able to make it clear to me just what you mean. I didn't have a golden childhood. I don't know anyone who had a golden childhood. What is the advantage of a golden childhood if it escapes you in your thirties and forties and is as forgotten as the language the cavemen spoke to one another? Are we all sentenced to looking for a Garden of Eden for the rest of our lives? Fuck that fable. Fuck the Garden of Eden. There was no Garden of Eden. It never existed. We are crazy to think this life is anything more than what it is. The people who paint pictures, write books, compose music, eat sunflower seeds, feed their children zucchini for breakfast, they think they are finding the Garden of Eden. I don't dream of a Garden of Eden. I wouldn't know what to do if I found the Garden of Eden. I am on a planet whirling in space and I don't know what lies one hundred billion light-years in front of me. I have a handful of words to explain three billion lives on this earth.

That there is no Garden of Eden, anywhere in the universe, keeps you awake at night, Elaine. You think that somewhere in this world is a land beyond the sea as Judy Garland might sing it, there is a world of the Garden of Eden that we look for all our life. You think this haunts our dreams and because we can't find it, because it seems to be as lost to us as our childhood memories, we won't settle for anything less. Fuck the lost Garden of Eden. The world is being able to pay the bill at the checkout counter of the Grand Union, to pay the fucking New York Telephone Company, to pay electric and gas bills that are now more expensive than money. I will not surrender myself to a fiction invented by sheepherders ten thousand years ago who didn't have the advantage of reading the *New York Times* every day. The only dream I will chase is a hamburger and French fries at McDonald's. Michael and I will talk about life and not death. Berg who jumped to his death was chasing a dream, a dream that life was more than it promised, and he found his dream in a broken body that will never rise up again from the pavement on 49th Street. To live is everything. Men have spent twenty years in solitary confinement and come out smiling and planted tomato gardens and even had children. Whenever I want to know what life is I walk through the wing of a hospital where men and women lie stretched out in iron lungs and smile at the nurses and blink their eyes in the sunlight that comes through the windows. Fuck chasing the dream of death. Elaine, you are chasing a dream that will get your head stuck on top of a pole.

I pay my bills and that is what I have been taught the world has been about for the past ten thousand years. I will be forty years old on August 18 and I still care about Michael winning the Blue Jay race. I cannot surrender. Here is the Garden of Eden: the conductor coming down the aisle who doesn't care if I am Jesus Christ or Michelangelo. He wants to see my commuter's ticket and he will throw me off the train if I don't have a ticket. Today is punch day. Punching commuter tickets is an honorable job. All jobs are honorable. We are all prisoners, that is why there is no one to accept our surrender, and suicide is only possible for humans.

Elaine, Elaine, do you know how many times riding this train I try to see past your elegant elusive way of holding yourself apart from the world as though you have already been to Jupiter and back? Do you know how many times I think about you as I ride this miserable hot stinking train under Grand Central Station, out of the tunnel into Harlem, then through the Bronx that is strangling to death, and then toward Westchester where a refugee population from Manhattan lives in houses vacated by aged Protestants who could no longer afford to pay their oil bills. I sit by this train window and watch you flash by me like a heroine in a Hitchcock movie. You are a strange, pagan woman.

You won't be satisfied until the last shovelful of dirt is thrown on your coffin and then you will still ask for more, more, more. What is the more that you think exists in this world? Tell me what it is. Where is it? I will find it. I will take a sabbatical from my job. I will ride a camel across the desert. I will climb the Himalayan mountains. I will sail the *Sea Islander* off the edge of the earth. What is the more, more, more, that you talk about in your sleep? I feel you talking in your sleep. It's like the moaning of the dead who can't stand the fit of their coffins, who want more air to breathe. The whimpers when you moan in your sleep come from a world I don't know. I don't wake you when you moan. I don't dare have sex with you when you moan. I might find a hundred strange men from other planets in you before me. We are all safe in bed. It is only a dream. I know when you awake you will pour me orange juice and refuse to serve me two fried eggs and instead give me a bowl of steaming Irish oatmeal that you simmered like your great-grandmother. You are a good wife, Elaine. You don't hiss at salesladies. You threw away the gourmet cookbook ten years ago. The house is clean. The rooms in our house have a simple flair that escapes the interior decorators at Bloomingdale's because they don't know how to shop garage sales like we do. No one can tell what we spent on our furniture, and the rooms will not collapse if we remove a painting from the wall. But what is this more, more, more, that you see, that you feel escapes us, that you feel is somewhere to be picked up like the black raspberries on the Block Island roads. If only the map was in your hand. Where did Captain Kidd bury his iron chest on Block Island? They hanged Captain Kidd in

Newport and he never told anyone where he buried his chest. We hanged God and he hasn't told us where he buried his Garden of Eden. You frighten me. You fucking pagan strange wife. You make me feel I will lie in my grave and miss something.

I do not know who lives in Pelham. The train is slowing up to discharge passengers in Pelham. I have never spoken to anyone from Pelham. I will probably never speak to anyone from Pelham. You see, Elaine, I don't miss Pelham, I do not have to know Pelham, I don't miss anything I don't experience. What is this inner world that you think glows like a red-hot atom, that you think I do not see, nor Michael? Do you think I am too Harvard graduate to see? I see, Elaine. We are all mystics. The Irish prove that to us. I love the Irish when they fly out of their skins and haunt the world with messages they receive from the other side of the mountain. I want to celebrate my fortieth birthday wearing a purple robe like a king. I want to sit in a pub and get drunk and sing old sea songs. I want to climb to the top of a fifty-foot mast and feed the sea gulls part of my birthday cake. I want to sail into the Atlantic and disappear into the fogbanks off of Newfoundland and sail to the king of us all. I want to fuck you as slowly as the second hand moves on a quartz watch. I want you to come like a teakettle left alone in the kitchen with no one to turn off the burner. I will be forty and God has let me see 14,500 days that I can't explain. When I am forty we will climb to the top of the big glacial rock in Manor Park and hold each other and shiver in the breeze as we realize life is overtaking us. Elaine, you will live with me, you will hold my hand when I am ready to die and tell me not to be afraid, and you will nod to the doctor and he will pull the plug and I will sink into death.

I see the train pulling into Larchmont, past the lumberyard, past the movie house, past the bridge, past the bakery, and I leave my seat by the window which gives me a reflection of myself and no other secrets.

I will not take a taxicab. I will not take the yellow bus for a quarter. I will walk. I do not need my suit from the cleaners. I will not pick up a barbecued chicken. I will take Michael and Elaine to a Chinese restaurant and the fortune cookie will tell Michael that he will win the Blue Jay race. I like walking to the house. I hate the leather-skinned ladies in their tennis dresses who pick up their husbands at the station as though they are doing ambulance duty for the Red Cross on the western front. Why don't they grab their husbands' cocks as they get into the cars and stick their hot tongues down into their husbands' ears and bring themselves off on the steering wheel? The cars wait at the station like a cortege. I will walk. I am always impressed by the ugliness of downtown Larchmont. It is deliberate. It is calculated. It is class. Larchmont is straight avenues, no-nonsense banks, an abundance of drugstores, always the sign of affluence. The *Mamaroneck Daily Times* found one slum in Larchmont in 1973 and that was burned to the ground, without the inhabitants in it.

Elaine, you are the one who is a mystery, not me. It is you who brought the *Sea Islander* through a storm into New Harbor on Block Island. It is you, not me, who sat out the fog and listened for the foghorns, and it was you who led us out of the fog that holds Block Island in a vise. It was you, not me, who dove into the Atlantic and grabbed Michael before the waves sucked him under when he tumbled overboard from the *Sea Islander*.

I like our house when I approach it on foot. I like the way our house sits on the ground, high on the ground. The white columns always remind me of Robert E. Lee. I like our great circular porch with the white wicker rocking chairs and the white wicker tea cart that we bought in Guilford. The deed says Stanford White designed the house. We have a sea town house, Elaine. I am the captain of a whaling ship and I am walking to the front door of our house after three years at sea hunting whales in the Indian Ocean. Where are the three-hundred-foot yachts that used to line Larchmont harbor? Where are the Japanese lanterns? In which Larchmont house did a Barrymore die? Do I hear voices singing sea chanteys? Whale ahead! Whale ahead! Lower the boats. I can see Michael in the Blue Jay and the sails filling with wind. I can hear the roar of the starter cannon. Let there be a strong wind. I never lock our front door. When we moved to Larchmont I believed no one locked their front door. Now everyone locks their front doors and the dogs howl at strangers and friends. The newsboy hasn't left the paper yet. Michael must be up in his room. Elaine is at home. I will go up to Michael's room and tell him that Sunday will be sunny with winds blowing at fifteen knots. That is the best wind for a Blue Jay. Do you hear, Michael: winds of fifteen knots and a sunny sky? The compass in Michael's room always points due north. Who is singing the sea chanteys? Who sighted the whale?

I opened the door to Michael's room.

Two

The Whirlwind

I ask a favor of you. I would like you to suspend judgment on what Philip saw when he opened the door to his son's bedroom. There is a reason for this request. I don't think the author can proceed with his story unless you suspend the judgment of ten thousand years, perhaps fifty thousand years. I know this is possible. I have done it. You have also done it in other matters, for you are enveloped in rules of behavior. Sometimes you suspect what you believe is right. You kill in war. You drop a bomb that kills 75,000 people in three seconds. That is a suspension of judgment. You allow the mentally ill to be locked in state hospitals without seeing a doctor from January to December. That is a suspension of judgment. You permit the retarded to wander naked through the corridors of their institutions and sit in their own shit and curl up like worms to sleep on cold floors. Men go to bed with other men's wives with less effort than they take to shave, and they feel proud of the act and quote Freud and *Cosmopolitan* magazine in support of their efforts. Larchmont housewives journey into the city on the 10:22 and go to bars in New York City that they know will lead to an afternoon in bed in a hotel room that gives them a glorious feeling they can never get in their remodeled kitchens. You permit 1,250,000 people to live on less than two dollars a day in New York City and that is a suspension of belief. You permit the aged to vegetate in nursing homes and only care about how much money the nursing home operators steal. That is a suspension of judgment. You permit eight million men to be unemployed. That is a suspension of judgment. You arm for a war that cannot last more than twenty minutes. That is a suspension of judgment. You killed the Vietnamese like lice. That was a suspension of judgment. I could go on and on. Most of life consists of a suspension of belief or judgment. This is why the mass of all men live in fear and anxiety.

What is there to believe, if the evidence is contrary to belief. You watch babies smile and later wonder where the smile has fled. You are more lonely than any tree. You are lonely when you are together and you wonder why, since it is hard to distinguish any differences away from you. You no longer hear what you say to one another because you have lost your own voice. You listen all your lives for the sound of a voice that will tell you who you are, for that can only come from another person, and everything seems to conspire against you hearing that voice.

It is a strange journey you are on. One wonders how the masses of mankind live on as they do. The strangest belief you hold is that one person can save you, and why this belief is spread over the entire world and why it has persisted for thousands of years is unknowable. I think what Philip saw and Elaine did is worthy of your suspension of judgment. It is an act that all the world considers heinous without knowing why they feel it is heinous, why they consider it loathsome. You can search the Harvard Library and come up with only a handful of books that have ever looked at this act. It was made loathsome and heinous in the days before we began to formulate words. It is not a question to be asked, for it begs an answer you dare not give. I am sure the critics will attack Elaine as though they have received their orders from the War Office. The critics in all epochs are fools who think they are defending me. You must understand they exist to keep you filled with stories and poems and movies and plays and legends that soften your mind, dull your wild sense of beauty, dull your dreams. Yes, you still have your own life in dreams. That world hasn't been invaded. That is where you escape like men trapped in a submarine at the bottom of the sea who rise through a hatch to the broad beauty of the sea. You could not live without your dreams. You would all march into the sea and drown yourselves. The critic cannot hold back the dream. I have said enough. Let the story begin. For a million years you have been telling one another stories. But there was a time in the beginning when there were no stories to tell, no fiction to invent about yourselves.

Philip

Where are the gods to save me! Hermes! Hercules! Homer! Moses! Buddha! Jesus! None of them are at my side! Freud! Kant! Spinoza! James! Emerson! Melville! They have all fled. Zeus. Why did they teach me that these were the gods to protect me? Where are they now? Why have they lasted so long? They are as dead as any other men. Why do we honor our dead when it is the living we must live with? Who is there among the living that we honor? I can't find a single name in all the editions of the *Times*. What did I learn from reading Tolstoy, all those evenings with strange Russian names. And Dostoevski, with his madness. After his books are read, what does he tell us? Kafka I remember. Kafka never believed life was right. There were missing pieces. Elaine never believed that I read Kafka. I was Kafka when I read Kafka. I wrote every line before Kafka wrote it. I could have proved it if I had tape-recorded myself as I was reading *The Trial*.

Beckett. Beckett would be my friend if we met. How does one meet Beckett? One never meets Beckett. I am a wild sea captain. I have crashed yawls against the rocks at Block Island. I have swum through the boiling, raging surf. I have gasped on the white sand and then climbed the cliffs of Mohegan's Bluff to begin again. I have raised a son to race across Long Island Sound, a son Elaine recovered from the sea when a wave flung him overboard. They both rose out of the waves laughing and gasping for breath and I brought the *Sea Islander* around and the three of us sat on deck as though we had outwitted all of existence. It seems the sea wants to reclaim Michael. Michael is not our child. Michael is on loan to us from the sea. The boiling sea will be his home for a billion years and that will seem like a morning at breakfast.

I opened the door to Michael's bedroom to tell him that winds of ten to fifteen knots were expected in the morning, rising to gusts of twenty. Elaine was mounted on top of him, her hair undone, her body shining in the dark as though covered with a luminous paint. I could see her eyes, they had a blue light, her hands on Michael's arms were covered with sweat, beaded, shining like blue diamonds, her nostrils were flared like the horses whipped by Hadrian, and she rose up and down on Michael like the earth trying to find itself in the days when the world was still a void. Elaine struck the balance as she turned to see me. She couldn't and didn't want to conceal the orgasm from me, it shook her body and contorted her face, she let out a moan that called to all of the booming surfs. The booming surfs answered her as she sank down on Michael and she didn't allow my standing in the door-

57

way to interfere with the resurgence of an orgasm that must have begun in her a hundred thousand years ago, for weren't we all born together? She luxuriated in her orgasm.

What about Michael? Michael looked at me the way every condemned prisoner must look at his hangman. Asking the forgiveness the condemned prisoner knows the hangman isn't able to give. I had already forgiven Michael. I forgave Michael a long time ago when he was born and I had reached an age when I knew forgiveness was not a luxury.

What did Michael do? Michael was prone on the bed, his hands on his mother's shoulders, his knees bent, his eyes were closed, he was pulling his mother down onto him, only the umbilical cord had been cut at 2:20 A.M. at Mt. Sinai Hospital, and he was alone in the embrace, as was his mother.

Michael said, "My God."

Elaine when she was able to speak, for she would not admit my presence until her orgasm had subsided, said, "I don't believe it, you came home early only once before from that office."

Then I moved. I pulled Elaine off Michael. I flung Elaine off the bed, hurling her against the wall. I went after Elaine, climbing over the bed, I picked up Elaine and slapped her across her mouth. Blood came out of her mouth and ran down her lower lip, to her breasts. She put up her hands to protect her face. I slapped her again and this time she flung out her hands to protect herself, digging her nails into my arms, pulling her nails down my arms, opening up two tracks of blood. I hurled Elaine against the wall again. Elaine put out her hands again to dig her nails into me. This time she went for my face, my eyes, and I slapped her hands away, twisting them behind her, and I bent her body to the floor, and when she lay there huddled up, I grabbed the blanket off the bed and covered her body as though she was a dead cat run over by a beer truck.

I turned to Michael and said, "Get dressed. Let us alone. Just let us alone."

Michael

What am I going to tell you? God didn't hurl any lightning bolts at me. The earth didn't shake. Larchmont didn't sink into the Sound. Boats weren't flung against the glacial rocks of Manor Beach Park. Our house didn't vanish into marshland. Do you want my deposition? Of course you do. How often do you have access to a son who has just been had by his mother.

It was past four. I saw the sun shift, the wind pick up. I figured my mother was coming in with the Blue Jay. The Sound can get black in a minute and the boat gets to be a hassle in a downpour. Sometimes even with the rain there is no wind and you just sit in the downpour, bailing out water and getting soaking wet. I think a lot about my mother. Not many sons will tell you this, but I think about the time I was in her stomach, or is it the womb.

At school there is a girl who writes long papers

about the time she was in her mother, the time before she was born but still alive. The papers run forty to fifty pages and she lets me read them. Amy writes with real ink and she writes in a small cribbed handwriting, so it's hard to read everything she writes. But what I could read was amazing. I know her mother. She bakes wonderful fresh bread. Amy describes being inside of her mother. The "life support system," Amy told me, "is something like the first astronauts', who looked like they were sitting in a womb." Amy said that she was completely tied to another person when she was inside her mother, and she knew it wouldn't last, and once she was out of her mother's life support system she would be on her own because, Amy said, "Nothing in this world is ever as perfect as the support you get when you are in the womb. It is all there, in the amounts you need, air, food, love, warmth, comfort, not being alone, words. You don't wonder where you are or why you are there. Some people say babies know everything before they are born and then an angel taps them on their forehead when they are born and they forget everything. We don't forget everything. We never forget our life in the womb. We don't think about it. We don't dare. That memory of being so protected is too hard for us to take. But nothing will ever convince me that we don't think about it. I do more than think about it. I can go back into that time and I can be that curled-up living thing that is me and will never be anything but me for all time. We have to learn to think about that kind of time, the time when we were inside of our mothers. It doesn't mean I had an identity then like being a doctor or a teacher or a painter, but I did have a feeling that I was linked to another person, and through that person linked to the entire universe, and I wasn't frightened, and why fears can begin as soon as life starts outside of the skin of another person is the mystery I don't understand."

I thought that was brilliant when Amy told it to me. When Amy and I are in bed, Amy says to me, "Can you touch the spot, can you feel the spot inside of me where it all begins, if I squeeze my legs tight do you feel it?" No, I would tell Amy, I don't feel it. She would squeeze her legs tighter and try to bring me inside of her, even the way she kissed, as though she could devour me. Screwing Amy is work. Amy wants all of you inside of her. Amy is too intense for this life. At school the teachers ignore her, and most of the time Amy is daydreaming or else bringing herself off by rubbing up against the desk or holding a book in her lap that serves the same purpose. I sometimes see her eyeballs roll around in her head and then squeeze tight. I tell you all this just to let you know that a fifteen-year-old boy is not altogether innocent. In Larchmont it would be hard to be innocent. The kids all seem to have a secret pipeline into their parents' bedrooms and they know the good and bad, just as cats and dogs learn their way around the house. I know my father and mother fight in bed. I hear them screaming at each other, the screams are followed by a long silence, and then I see my father leaving the bedroom and going downstairs to turn on the TV and stuff himself with ice-cold honeydew melon. I once read in a book that the French whorehouses had peepholes where customers could look at other customers screwing. I have a peephole to my parents' bedroom, only it isn't a hole in the wall but an ear to the wall.

By putting my ear against the wall I can hear what they are saying. That is more exciting to me than watching them screwing. The wall seems to be a natural conductor of sound. Their voices come through just as though I was hearing them on a cassette tape recorder. I understand I can buy a piece of equipment for my tape recorder that I can press against the wall and it will pick up voices on the other side and record them. I wonder if the words would have the same meaning on tape? This is a for example. My mother: Don't touch me now, you always want to touch when I'm reading the newspaper. My father: Fuck the newspaper. Turn on your side. My mother: I won't. Go read a book. My father: I said turn on your side. My mother: I have a right to be fucked when I want to be, not when you want to. My father: Am I going to hear that crap for the rest of my life. My mother: All right, do it if you want to, but I am going to keep on reading the newspaper. My father: If you read that paper while I'm fucking you I'll shove that paper down your throat. My mother: I don't care what you do. Just get it over with. My father: It is over with. Go fuck yourself. My mother: You have a filthy mouth. My father: I learned it from you, dear, all from you. This would all be followed by a silence, then the running of water in the bathroom. I figure they needed those scenes to work themselves up.

I just finished *The Brothers Karamazov* by Dostoevski. I wish I could deliver a speech like the defense lawyer at the end of the book which is so brilliant that you don't know how it was put together. But I don't see what I have to defend yet. Amy has taught me a hell of a lot. Amy said to me when we were in her bed on

Orienta Point: "I will not feel guilty for anything or anybody. This world was all here before I was put into it. I didn't feel guilty in that other world when I was inside of my mother. I didn't recognize my mother when I came out of her. She was an entirely different person. She didn't hold me. She didn't cuddle me. She didn't kiss me. She didn't let me feel the warmth of her body. My father looked at me like I was some toy he'd brought home from F.A.O. Schwarz. He filled my room with toys. I couldn't move on the floor or climb onto my bed without going over tons of toys. I didn't have any room for my own life. It was all filled with those useless toys. I loved to walk down to the water and see the millions of little fish swimming almost on the shore and it dazzled me that each one of those fish had a separate life of its own and in all that water and among all those fish it could find its own mother. I loved to watch the birds. I loved it in the fall when I would look up and suddenly see a flock of birds flying south. Those V formations of geese were breathtaking. My father should have known that I didn't need all those toys."

I liked Amy saying she didn't feel guilty about anything because she came into the world when it was all put together and she had no say in how anything was put together. I was innocent all through my childhood from the day I was born, Amy would say. Innocent.

I do not believe being born makes us innocent. There I part company with Amy. None of us are innocent. This is why we need man-made laws to judge us. When we come into the world, the world is changed by our presence. My presence means something in this world. My presence has altered the way my mother and father feel about each other. My presence shocked them into realizing they gave birth to life. My presence made them realize that life is not a game or a dream. They had to keep me alive or else they would be murderers. I know kids in Larchmont who are afraid of their parents. Take Allen Kennedy. He tells me that he is afraid to go to sleep at night because he believes his father is going to come into his bedroom and strangle him. Allen Kennedy really believes his father is going to kill him. I suggested that he see the psychologist at school or a shrink. "If I believe my father is going to kill me, then that is worse than him killing me," Allen Kennedy tells me.

We are not innocent from the day of our birth. We need a crib. We need food. We need water, milk. We need clothes. We need love. We need warmth. We need to be protected from too much heat, the cold. We need to be protected from death. Babies die mysterious crib deaths. The blankets suffocate babies to death. Babies catch their heads between the railing and strangle to death. Some babies fall out of the crib and smash their heads. Babies choke on food. Babies need their diapers changed or they develop sores. Babies need doctors. They need vitamins. Babies cry and demand attention. Babies are not innocent. Babies are part of life the minute they are exposed to the air. Babies are not helpless playthings. My mother tells me that I had to be rushed to the hospital at three in the morning when I was turning blue and she kept screaming don't let him die, don't let him die. She said my father drove the car at eighty miles an hour to the New Rochelle Hospital emergency room.

We all seem so alike. Then what is it that makes us

different? How am I different from Amy or Allen Kennedy? Why should I be different? What advantage is there to us in being different? Wouldn't we be better off if we were all the same? Then we would be sure about our feelings. We wouldn't be so confused. We would know where we stand, who we are, instead of always trying to imagine who we are, waiting for a Homer or a Shakespeare to give us a name or a face. I do not believe we are so different. We use the same language but, believe me, we don't all mean the same thing when we say the same words. Maybe it is language that makes us different. Maybe it is in words that we hide from one another. Words are the most mysterious invention of mankind. I went through the *Encyclopaedia Britannica* trying to find out how words came into existence. But nobody knows. How do we make words? How did we begin to give meaning to words? What are all the things we give names to? How do we know the names are right? How do we know the translations we read are right? How can I be sure that I am reading what Homer said and not what some Englishman is saying who translates Homer? Why do we have so many languages? I know my mother's language. My God, she has a special language, filled with meaning more difficult to understand than the most complicated math they can throw at you at Mamaroneck High School. My mother gives her own meaning to words, things, life, objects, me, my father, herself, our cat. She doesn't care about logic. Things are true when she wants them to be true, otherwise they aren't true. My mother hasn't understood this game yet. It drives my father nuts. It makes him stop talking to my mother. She screams, "We don't communicate." He screams back, "I'd rather communicate to a horse." It doesn't make sense. We make our lives a babel with words. Think of that most mysterious of all phrases, I love you. Amy says we build and rebuild our lives on those three words like ants carrying scraps of food to their anthills.

You are waiting for a deposition. Will you understand it? Will you listen to my words or your words? Have you already made up your mind about me? How can I convince you that I am me? For purposes of understanding between us, you must believe I am me. To listen to me, you must care about me. To hear me, you must know me. To really listen to me, you must believe I am somehow a part of your world. We hide from strangers. We ignore people not like ourselves. This is why Amy doesn't have a friend at Mamaroneck except me. I listen to Amy because I believe she is on to something important.

If you could see me for an afternoon on the Blue Jay, you would see how efficient I am on the boat. I know every line, bolt, screw, rope on the boat. I know the sky, the different colors of the Sound, the sun, the winds. The boat responds to me. We work together to use the wind. I never have to fight the boat. I never curse it. I never curse the wind or the sky. I never yell at the sun. I don't care if it rains, or if a storm comes up. This is the way I think life should be and the way it is on good days. I see it in my father's face when he has a good day. I see it in my mother's face when she comes out of the bedroom humming. But the boat isn't my whole life. I like to read Charles Dickens. I like to talk to Amy. I like some of my teachers, particularly the science teacher, Dr. Fowles, who keeps telling us that if we ever understand one of the puzzles of the universe, just one, like gravity or electricity or motion or atoms, it will all come together like a pie and "we will see into the dawn of the world." Dr. Fowles says this with the window open and the sun shining on his face, his hands stuck into the pockets of his tweed jacket. "Read the letters of Sean O'Casey, that's a science, to communicate yourself in a letter like O'Casey," he tells us. Once in a great while from a teacher you get a glimmer of more than knowledge. I hope you get a glimmer from me of more than what you think I am.

I like my father. But he does some crazy things. Sometimes we go out to the golf driving range together in Scarsdale. He gets a big bucket of golf balls for $2.50. He's not hitting the golf balls, he's hitting my mother in the head with that shiny steel golf club every time he swings. Fuck you, you dirty bitch, I hear him say, and then he swings the golf club with a desperate hope that he will slam the ball into infinity. I asked my father why he curses when he swings the golf club. My father said something I liked, which I repeated to Amy: "Cursing is the only prayer most of us know." Now I understand why my mother curses so much.

My mother has her own game that she plays with my father. When my father comes home from riding that Penn Central train that everybody hates, he comes into the kitchen and expects a big hello from my mother for riding that train, and she gives him a cold icy stare that makes him turn on his heels and slink out of the kitchen like an unhappy dog that has just been cursed out.

I wonder why people don't explore one another more than they do. I mean my mother and father, for example. There's so much they could talk about, so much they could tell each other, so many questions they could ask each other, so many stories from the past, so much history from the family, because occasionally they do relax and I love to hear them tell stories about the old days and the way they met. I've been living with my parents for fifteen years and I know very little about them. I know nothing about my father's old girl friends, for example. I know nothing about any of the men my mother may have fucked before she met my father, except for Dr. Fields. I don't know where my father took my mother on dates in New York City. I would like to see some of those places. Once in a while they mention Greenwich Village like it was something out of *The Great Gatsby.*

I went to the Village with Amy and all we saw were black men stretched out on the park benches in Washington Square stroking their thighs and cupping their cocks. The sidewalks were dirty. Everybody seemed to have a vacant stare on his face.

We went to see the house on Bank Street where my mother lived for a couple of years. It was a brownstone with big windows on the ground floor and a nice wrought-iron fence. We rang the doorbell and a super came to the door. I said my mother used to live in this house and could we just go inside for a minute. The super said, "Sure, kid." I was wearing a Lacoste shirt and Top-Siders so he knew I was all right. We went into the foyer. The brownstone smelled like an old house. I saw a curved stairway. My mother said she lived on the second floor. I asked if we could go up one

69

flight of stairs. The super said, "Sure, kid." The stairs were carpeted with a green rug. The walls were painted brown. From the second-floor landing I saw my mother's old room, 2FR. I got a little sexy. The door to her room was big and heavy like in the old Larchmont houses. The door opened into my mother's old room. This is where her old boyfriends came to see her. The room had a studio couch, white curtains, a tiny kitchen—my mother remembered the striped Indian throw on the studio couch, the tiny kitchen and the huge bathroom. This was the room where all kinds of guys must have gotten into my mother, or so she lets my father think when she wants to needle him. I could see her younger and stretched out on the studio couch all hot and sweating and a guy with his pants off getting into her. Any one of those guys could have been my father. My mother must have liked to fuck in that room. Certainly more than she likes to fuck in her room in Larchmont. Each house should have a room of memories. The room should be filled with pictures, posters, toys, games, letters, clothes, all filled with memories from the past. You should be able to go there to recollect yourself, instead of collecting other people's junk like the crazy ladies do in Larchmont who run from one garage sale to another like they'll miss something. People should collect themselves. That's what I am going to start doing. Nothing remains in my room unless it is a part of my past. The collecting room. A room of memories. A room for me. I wanted to go into my mother's old room in that brownstone. I asked Amy if we should knock on the door. Amy said, "Sure."

I knocked. We waited. We heard somebody moving.

The door opened on a chain. I saw a frightened face. It was a girl about twenty-five. "Yes?" she said, as though I had been summoned to murder her. "My mother used to live in this room," I said. "Oh," she said, relaxed to see that I wasn't a murderer. "Can we see the room?" I asked. She studied us through the chain. I could see her thinking, if these kids are murderers and thieves then there's no escape and I might as well have it happen now. She opened the door. I saw the studio couch. I saw the tiny kitchen. I saw the white curtains. I saw the Indian bedspread, reds, blues, a deep pink. I saw my mother coming out of the big bathroom naked except for a towel wrapped around her head, and then I saw her drop the towel and stretch out on the bed and raise up her legs and I could see the place where I had lived for nine months of my life, that deep, deep inside of her, and I could see myself on top of her trying to force myself back in her because deep, deep inside of her was an incredible warmth, a softness, a clinging like a tree to the earth, deep, deep, was all I could think, deep like looking into the sky, deep like going to sleep and knowing you would wake up in the morning, deep like when we are all relaxed around the dinner table, deep with me extended into Amy, pushing into Amy as though there was a button inside of her that I could touch that would open up all the doors, but that wasn't in Amy but in my mother, that world of whirling lights and great sounds and great silences and great warmth and great love and great feeling all over, that feeling that nothing else was as important as this warmth and comfort, that I could never find it anywhere else. I went over to the studio bed and lay down on top of that

Indian cover and for an instant, just for an instant, before the girl yelled *what are you doing on my bed,* I felt myself inside of my mother, and in that microsecond, it couldn't have been more than a thousandth part of a second, I saw the whole world clearer than a tennis ball, and I knew that everything in the world was somehow connected to that feeling inside of my mother, the feeling that we give life to one another, and for a period in every life, whether the life of a bee, a cat, a lion, a bear, a horse, or us, we are protected. The girl almost pulled me off the bed as though I was about to defile it. She said you have to leave, you have to leave, and that frightened look came over her face and I knew I could never explain to her how much I owed her for that microsecond of time.

So you see, I wasn't entirely unprepared when my mother walked into my bedroom with a towel wrapped around her head and said, "I get so worked up taking the Blue Jay out. Can I lie down next to you for a second." When we kissed I knew why people kissed. It was to get back to that first embrace. My mother's kiss was just that. I had never felt anything so delicious. When she mounted herself on top of me I never had seen a face so deep back into itself, as though it was watching a Fourth of July celebration at the beginning of the world. When she sank herself down on me it was as though we were both slipping off into a dream that we had both dreamed a million times. I couldn't be sure of what my mother was thinking except that she didn't talk and she did everything without showing, whether she felt it was right or wrong or just something that had to be done. I went all of the way inside of her and touched something delicious and that was when I shuddered, just as I shuddered when I was born and brought into this world. I know now what an orgasm is.

I felt torn apart when I looked up and saw my father's tortured face. I burst into a thousand pieces. It was like someone swung me by my feet against the wall. No son should ever see his father's face like that, like the skin that gave him his face was ripped off and there was nothing left but a hollow skeleton with no face. For an instant, less than an instant, we stared at one another, and I did not understand my father well enough yet to know what the look meant.

Elaine, Philip, the Whirlwind

"Can we talk now?" Elaine asked.

"About what?" Philip asked.

"About what you saw. Do you want to talk about it or do you want to hit me again?"

"I'm not going to hit you again. I'm not going to hit anybody. I'm just going to get the hell out of here and get a room at the Drake."

"Can't you ever stop being a fool?"

"That's absolutely right. I am a fool. A big fucking fool."

"Why don't you put some Bacitracin on those scratches?"

"I will. I need more than Bacitracin."

"I'll get it."

"No, you won't. I don't want a fucking thing from you."

"You are going to be a fool."

"Yes, I'm going to be a fool. Until I forget that look on Michael's face I'm going to be a fool. Do you think I give a shit about you?"

"Maybe it was the look on your face that Michael has to forget."

"Look, I can't turn the clock back. Michael can't turn the clock back. It happened. But it's not going to happen again. If I had a brain in my head I would call the Larchmont police and have you picked up. That's a Class E felony in New York."

"So is someone sucking your dick."

"You're trying to tell me something. What is it?"

"Do you want to listen?"

"No, I don't want to listen. What can you tell me that is different from what I saw? About two hours ago we were a family. A fucked-up, screwed-up family, but we were a family. We bought food at the Grand Union. We ate dinner together. Sometimes we talked like a family. Sometimes we even fucked like a man and wife. We made it, as the kids say. But you fucked that out the window. Now you can join those Larchmont cunts with their divorces."

"So you think that's the way out of this?"

"The way out of what I just saw is to forget it. Just like we forget the corpse that we see at burials. The corpse is out of our heads the minute we see the sun shining and people walking on the sidewalk. The minute I leave you the fucking sun will shine. You want to fuck your son, fine, the next time you try it I'll have you dragged away from here into an ambulance headed for a state hospital."

"Then there's nothing for us to talk about."

"You're absolutely right."

"When are you leaving?"

"After the race."

"You still want Michael to win the race."

"I think he has to win that race now."

"And if he loses?"

"It doesn't take a lot to be a loser today. I don't see Michael as any bigger or brighter than any of the kids he brings into the house. I just think he needs a lift. God, does he need a lift now. Winning the Blue Jay race will probably give him the lift he needs. Why am I talking to you? I should be slamming your fucking head against the wall. Look, get the hell out of this room, stay the fuck away from me, don't bring up this subject again. In about a week you'll get a letter from my lawyer. In three weeks if you don't have any serious objections I can fly down to Haiti and get a divorce in three hours and you can live with this thing but I won't. I'll take Michael the hell out of here and we'll find an apartment in the city where nobody knows us and nobody cares who we are. As for you, you can buy yourself a vibrator with your settlement money and fuck yourself to death. There isn't a judge in the universe who would give you custody of Michael. For about a three-second orgasm you blew it. Fine. I hope you enjoyed yourself. I don't think you'll find it was worth it."

"You don't know a thing about it."

"Thank you, I don't want to. There's a lot I don't know about. What I don't know doesn't bother me."

"You're not the least bit interested in knowing why I did what I did with Michael? You don't want to hear me say it?"

"Everybody thinks he's right. Murderers think they

are right when they kill. Muggers think they are right when they steal. The guy who takes money from the blind news dealer feels it's coming to him. Whatever you tell me will make it right for you, wrong for me, good for Michael. Jesus, do you think I am one of those Larchmont men who can only read the financial page and nothing else. I know a little bit about the history of this world. I know that in most of the countries of this world they would have already chopped your head off. You have no explanation. You just have a bunch of words that you want to call up in your defense that don't mean shit in the real world. In the real world you are a cunt who fucked her son, who probably ruined him for life, and why you did it doesn't mean anything. It's not something we can forget like some of those crazy arguments we have."

"I would think you would want to hear what I have to say."

"Send me a letter."

"You're afraid to hear what I have to say."

"I am afraid I may strangle you. Or beat you to death. Like Nixon I have a fear of prisons."

"Like most men you have a fear of what your wife will tell you."

"I stopped believing in my immortality the day I took out a loan from First National City Bank to buy a Dodge Dart. Look Elaine, I realize this happened in our house, in Michael's bedroom, and we were the only witnesses unless God had nothing better to do between five and five-thirty. It doesn't have to leave this room. I'm not going to call in the Larchmont reform Democrats and ask them for their opinion. I'm not going to write to the daily help column. I am just going to get as far away from you as I can and try to forget that we ever had a happy day between us. If St. Augustine and George Bernard Shaw defended you I wouldn't care. We have a secret between us. Michael has a secret. I am sure he won't broadcast it in the pizza parlors of Mamaroneck. I simply do not believe that you and I can live together after this, and rather than scream and shout I am going to ask you to leave me alone. I don't want to see your face at breakfast. I don't want you sleeping next to me. I don't believe you and I and Michael can sit down to breakfast or dinner or even in front of the TV set again. Do you realize what you have done? You have made it impossible for your son to know that he has a mother. A divorce between us would be nothing, it happens every thirty-eight minutes in Larchmont. But a divorce between a mother and her son is another matter. I have said my little piece. I think I have exhausted all of the conventional wisdom on the subject. It is not something one can talk about as you obviously want to do. It is an act that one obliterates, just as one obliterates a bad dream. I am going to sit down with a bottle of Jack Daniels and try a little obliteration. What I am really trying to do is to keep cool and avoid a heart attack, and if I don't get out of this room I may be at the mercy of all those blood vessels in my head that seem ready to pop open. For a moment in that room you did look like a wild heroine. I wonder if the martyrs felt that their cry of exaltation was worth the burning. Good night Elaine, you are right in a way, I do want to know why you did it, but I will never let you tell me.''

Three

Saturday Morning

Philip woke and crept out of the house. He couldn't recall his dreams and he wouldn't dare. For a brief moment he remembered lapsing into sleep as though he had been sentenced to death, stood against a shabby brick wall, shot by an unflinching firing squad, the order immediately carried out, the bullets splattering into him like the scenes in those old movies of Ronald Coleman. Was that the late late movie he tried to watch at 4 A.M.? It was a cool crisp Saturday morning. He had put on an old pair of denims, his Top-Siders, an old cotton T-shirt worn to the feel of silk, his Lee denim jacket which he wore every Saturday like an actor taping a beard to his face to play King Lear. He knew his route like an old milk horse. First to the bakery to buy fresh rolls, to glance at the *New York Times* without buying a copy because Saturday belonged to him. He would walk through the hardware store on the Boston Post Road looking for some gadget to buy like the new miracle glues that he could never get to work like the old glues. He would pass the ship's store and wonder as on every Saturday if he was ready for a new pair of Top-Siders. He knew Sunday sailors in Larchmont who held their Top-Siders together with adhesive tape. It seemed a point of honor not to abandon your Top-Siders.

He turned toward the water instead of the bakery shop on Chatsworth, since there would not be the usual Saturday morning breakfast of fresh rolls and cream cheese. Elaine was still asleep. He didn't dare face Michael. For a moment he had a crazy picture of Elaine, himself, and Michael eating breakfast in shifts, since they wouldn't know how to face one another as they had in the past, with that miraculous inexhaustible flow of conversation that made breakfast a delight and established their right to be called a family.

He wanted the water. He wanted to see only sky and water. He crossed over into Manor Beach Park and stepped on the grass as though he was entering a safer world. How wise it was to keep a stretch of Long Island Sound inviolate, to permit a park to grow where land sold for $100,000 an acre, to let the glacial rocks remain where nature had placed them, where children could see starfish sleeping on the rocks, where the elderly could sit and study the universe they would inhabit when they died. He was full of sadness for himself, since he knew no one in Larchmont he could talk to about Elaine's violation of their home, which was the only way he could think of yesterday afternoon.

He stared at the gray water of the Sound as though

looking for a bottle bobbing up that might contain a genie. If he ever wanted a genie to come out of the sea and offer him three wishes it was now. Certainly in inventing the story the Arabs had some feeling the past could be tampered with, that events could be altered, that the surface of the world could be peeled away like old wallpaper. Or maybe the Arabs were saying the past could no more be altered than a genie could be found in a bottle. In the *Arabian Nights* he remembered how the three wishes always wound up being worse than what the storyteller wanted wished away. How did the notion of wishing ever come into the human mind? He would check the *Oxford Universal Dictionary* that he had bought for eighty-five cents at a tag sale on Oak Avenue. He had spent part of the night searching through the medical, legal, anthropological books he had in the house, even the Bible, for information on the act Elaine had committed—that was the phrase, it was an act one committed—but the books told him nothing more than what he already knew. The *Columbia Encyclopedia* gave only twenty lines to incest when the world gave it its full measure of horror.

The Blue Jays swayed in the water off Horseshoe Harbor. He had learned to sail in an old Blue Jay when growing up in Great Neck, his father happy to have him handle the fourteen-foot sailboat with ease, and when he was thirteen his father solemnly presented him with a new Blue Jay. He should have kept the old one. The best memory he had of his father was sold for $350. His father crewed on the Bermuda races. His father was on the winning crew that raced to Newport. Philip remembered walking with his mother through the old streets of Newport, the houses that looked like history books, while they waited for his father's boat to come full sail in sight of Newport. He had always liked sailing into Block Island with his father because his father made Block Island seem like a fabled place, standing alone in the Atlantic, swept by winds throughout the winter, the trees leveled, leaving a wilderness shrubbery that was now being subdivided out of existence. They used to climb down the cliffs at Mohegan's Bluff and walk for miles on the wild beach. He and his father would sail into Block Island as though they had been at sea for years. His father would never enter New Harbor with the engines going, but always under sail. It was a cheap shot the way his father died, snatched away by a heart attack that didn't give him a chance to fight back, that strangled his father's heart in one terrible second, catching him alone in an elevator on the thirty-eighth floor of the building on Wall Street where he had his law firm. When the elevator doors opened on the thirty-eighth floor his secretary going down to Chock Full O' Nuts for a sandwich found him already dead.

Philip was catching up to the age his father was when he died. He often wondered if he would pass his father's age, a thought he knew he should drive out of his mind, but it persisted like an old scar. He had no father he could call on the phone and say let's meet at the Biltmore for lunch and talk. His father always understood what he meant by the word talk, it was a code word between them which meant nothing would be concealed.

Whom would he talk to in Larchmont where everyone smiled at you as though he faintly remembered you from a class reunion? Certainly not the men he knew at the Club who didn't want to be reminded of anything except the joy of being in a place where the robber barons ruled in the early days of the twentieth century. He never knew why he joined the Club except that he and his father would often drop anchor in Larchmont and take the launch to the Club where they had reciprocal privileges, and his father would show him the portraits of the past commodores and the splendid paintings of the old ships and tell him about the days when Larchmont harbor looked as glorious as the British Empire at the height of its Victorian grandeur, the days when the middle class believed the world had come to fruition for them and everything in the world was for their pleasure. How different it was today when the middle class felt itself being liquidated by taxes and even men making fifty thousand a year complained about their electric bills and their telephone bills.

When he first moved to Larchmont he believed he would find a small group of men he could talk to on Saturday mornings, men in whom he might dare confide without the risk of gossip or ridicule, but it didn't happen. He made few friends in Larchmont, and those mostly traveling companions on the Penn Central. He quickly learned he was like all the other men in Larchmont. Their decisions were made in New York. Their vocabulary was New York. Their contacts were in New York. Larchmont was a place where they stumbled home at night like punch-drunk fighters, looking for their English Tudors so they could get an overnight rest for the next day's onslaught. Inviting neighbors over for a drink, dinner, supper, snacks was like working a sixteen-hour day, and the gossip wasn't worth the effort. He tried to stay away from the obligatory parties in Larchmont where fifty to sixty people were brought together like rug merchants at an auction sale. A year's obligations were discharged in a single night. He always left those parties swearing he would never go to another. Elaine insisted on giving the same kind of party, and he never realized how many people he did know in Larchmont until he saw them all crowd into his house and look at him as though they weren't sure he was the host.

He was alone, that much he could document about himself.

He watched the water slowly change from gray to blue. The sun was breaking up the early morning mist on the water. It was the time of day he liked best, when everything seemed to be born again, just in case one had missed the sky and the water the day before. Offshore he could see their *Sea Islander* and Blue Jay. The *Sea Islander* was a brilliant white. Why didn't they sail the *Sea Islander* to Florida, or the Caribbean or Europe if they dared, instead of hugging the Connecticut coastline on Sunday day sails. His father had been more of a sailor than he would ever be. He never wanted to escape from the land as his father did. His father had been aboard a destroyer during the Battle of Midway and he would have stayed on in the Navy, but the Navy was no place for a Harvard law graduate.

He would get nowhere remembering his father who was now dead and unable to help him.

Philip walked along the rocky edge of the Larchmont shoreline on the magnificent glacial rocks which would have looked breathtaking in the South of

France. In Larchmont they were part of the endowment the town kept to itself while the other Westchester communities surrendered to shopping malls and pizza parlors. He knew from the book exhibits at the library that Larchmont had more authors than any town in the nation, but where were they? He didn't know a novelist in Larchmont, though Elaine said half of the houses in the Manor were wallpapered with galley proofs. He knew some doctors who practiced in New York, some lawyers who carried tennis rackets into the city, some TV producers who dressed like cowhands, a documentary filmmaker who would sink into meditation on the train. These he called his train friends, and they rode every morning together on the fantasy train that carried them into Manhattan where they labored like old-time prospectors in the Yukon.

On a stone bench which local legend said had been designed by Olmsted, the architect who laid out Manor Park and Central Park, Philip saw one of the few men in Larchmont he could call his friend, George Harris. Harris was a Madison Avenue publishing lawyer who had always wanted to teach legal philosophy at Amherst and who was now sending out feelers to the eastern universities. They had about as much use for him as a philosophy professor as they had for a permanent ballet company. Harris kept telling Philip he wanted to give up his law practice, but instead he began undoing his tie on the train and wearing wheat-colored corduroy trousers with a blue blazer. They usually came home together on the 5:15, a train Philip wished he would have caught yesterday. Elaine would never have dared then to tell him what she had done.

He waved to George Harris who waved back.

"Sit down," Harris said, making room on the bench, "and see what God has wrought. Why are you out earlier than me? This isn't your usual Saturday morning tour of Larchmont."

Should he step into the opening line like an actor who has been waiting hours to get on stage? He decided Harris was no more ready to hear what he had to say than to give him mouth-to-mouth resuscitation if he suddenly had a heart attack.

"I'm thinking of sailing to Block Island." He wasn't thinking of sailing to Block Island. Why did he say that?

"It's a great sail. We did it last year for the first time, but I couldn't stand those powerboats anchored end to end at New Harbor and Old Harbor where everybody seems to have their mouth clamped to a can of beer. Now tell me why you're up so early. Are your taxes being audited?"

"I'm too honest with my taxes. I got up early. Our friendly raccoon was knocking over the garbage cans. Did you ever get rid of the raccoons you had living in your attic?"

"They're gone and so is the five hundred dollars it took to get rid of them. I couldn't sleep last night either. I've been sitting here since eight, since the sign says the park opens at seven."

"Just your usual not being able to sleep or something special?" Philip asked.

"As usual I had a third of a bottle of Courvoisier, two Valiums and one late movie, this time Bette Davis in *Dangerous Lady,* and all that couldn't put me to sleep. It's just Pat again. Every day in every way she gives me another reason for leaving her. I have enough reasons now to divorce a dozen wives. This month she ran the telephone bill up to one hundred and seventy-five dollars calling her mother in Florida who lives in a semidetached retirement home which Pat says we may inherit one day and I say over my dead body. I suppose it's cheaper to call Florida than to fly there every weekend. But I hate the New York Telephone Company more than I hate doctors. I'd rather burn that money than pay it to the phone company. How do you explain the fact that the basic necessities of life have now become the most expensive. Phone bills, electricity, gas, the price of fuel oil, a visit to a doctor, even public transportation have become luxury items. It has me mixed up and makes me feel like a fool. I can't complain to Pat because she says in that brick-wall way of hers, what can you do but pay the bills if you want to live in Larchmont? Do you know what I really want to do? Leave Larchmont. I want to move West. I want to move to one of those towns about a hundred miles from Denver and renovate one of those old Victorian houses facing the Rockies and let Grand Central Station become as remote to me as the Roman baths. I don't know what keeps me from doing it except naked fear. You're not listening to a word I'm saying, are you? You still didn't tell me why you're up so early. I told you why I'm here."

"Walking." He couldn't tell Harris. Harris would immediately send him to a divorce lawyer—"bombers" Harris called them, because they are needed when you want to blow apart the deadwood of your marriage. Harris would die still talking about divorcing Pat. Harris would never leave Pat because he believed he had invested too much of his life in her—it would be like giving up a pension plan, Harris had once told him—and besides Pat was too old now to have the affairs that would have scared the hell out of him ten years ago.

"There's our Blue Jay," Philip said, pointing out the boat Michael would race, as though Harris had never seen the Blue Jay before.

"Will Michael win the first time out?"

"I think he will race to win." Philip heard his words betraying him, and he stood up as though the Blue Jay had broken loose from its mooring.

"You have troubles," Harris said.

"Yes, I have troubles," Philip said.

"Anything you want to talk about now?"

"Not now," Philip said.

"You know I can listen," Harris said.

But can you understand? Philip didn't dare ask the question. Harris also had a fifteen-year-old son.

"It's nothing I want to talk about now," Philip said.

"You do want to talk about it but you don't want to," Harris said. "I know the difference. We've talked about everything else. Tell me and I'll take a lawyer's oath of confidentiality, if necessary."

The quid pro quo was what he didn't like about Harris. Harris always insisted on "exchanging" information about their married lives. Philip liked to keep his married life with Elaine somewhat of a mystery, which it was anyhow, and Harris always accused him of holding back information. Of course he did. Life was the little mysteries. Wasn't it the highest degree of friendship when a friend never "demanded" anything of you?

"Walking back to the village?" Philip asked. "I can't

break the habit of picking up fresh rolls on Saturday."

"No, I'm just going to sit here and let the tide get up to around my ears before I start calling for help. Use the telephone and don't be a fool." Harris had reference to their mutual friend Bob Woods who hadn't phoned them to say that he was going to drive his car into a tree on the Boston Post Road at eighty miles an hour. A beer at the Larchmont Tavern might have saved his life.

Philip walked out of Manor Park. He walked slowly as though expecting Michael to run out of their house around the corner and tell him everything was all right, it was all right for him to return, yesterday had never happened. Michael didn't overtake him. There was no messenger. There would be no messenger. He walked across Fountain Square where Harris had bought his house in 1967 for $36,000, a house now worth $135,000, enough money for Harris to buy his Victorian house facing the Rockies. He walked up Grove Avenue past the house of one writer he'd met, a man whose book he had bought at Anderson's and which the writer had autographed with a green ball-point pen.

Philip was surprised that Elaine had never found a boyfriend in town, the men of Larchmont being far more attractive than the women, and far more interesting. He had heard about key parties in Larchmont, couples who sniffed cocaine, a famous actor who lived on hashish, but they were only stories talked about on the Penn Central. There were, he supposed, Larchmont parties where modest orgies took place, but he had never been invited, nor had anyone else he knew. The one experience he'd had with scandal was a party where marijuana cookies were served and the wife of a producer from CBS wore a blouse that revealed her delicate rose-colored nipples. How he could topple them all! How innocent all scandal seemed now! How he wanted to find a quiet place to weep. How he wanted to cry and have people come up to him and ask him if anything was wrong, could they go for something, could they be his father and mother and wife and son and the whole long line of the human race that had seemed to desert him this Saturday morning.

Maybe Elaine was right in some of the things she talked about so much, talking as though he would never understand. Things like childhood amnesia. He could feel at times that longing to recover his earliest memory of days that he couldn't find anymore in his mind, days which must have been pleasant and harmonious, because how else could babies be born if the experience was not pleasant and harmonious; nature would have found out a way of cutting off the experience if it was bad. How were all those babies born before Johns Hopkins Hospital and Columbia Presbyterian if birth wasn't harmonious with nature? How did we survive before Blue Cross and Blue Shield?

Elaine kept her thoughts to herself, and when she ventured an opinion at a Larchmont party she was usually hooted down by the doctors, psychiatrists, social workers, lawyers, stock brokers, tax lawyers, and schoolteachers as a housewife who wasn't entitled to an opinion that experts should express. He liked the way Elaine retreated at those times like a general who knows he has read the enemy's plans and realizes he has already won the battle, if not the victory.

He looked into the antique-shop windows on the

Boston Post Road and felt he should be on display and not the assortment of old oak chests and oak tables that seemed to be all there was left of American antiques for sale in Larchmont. He was an honest American antique in his worn blue denim pants, his worn blue T-shirt, his worn Top-Siders, his hope of finding comfort in the past when the future was the only place to find any comfort. During the long night he had used up every antique dirty word and every antique argument against Elaine. The dirty words seemed so quickly used up and he had no new language for cursing. He could not hide behind language. It was all out there in the open. He was the antique. That notion seemed to give him comfort. Objects became antiques overnight. Anything not in current production became an antique. People were antique from birth. They inherited a past that was already antique. Babies were antique from birth. No, they were not, Elaine would say, babies come into the world fresh and howling with the joy of being alive, not afraid of losing the comfort of the womb, of seeing the sunlight. Elaine said one only had to see a happy baby to know they experienced a happiness we could no longer comprehend. We need comedians to make us laugh. Babies laugh at the pleasure of participating in experiences, not avoiding experiences. How did Elaine know all this!

Philip hurried along the Boston Post Road, turning up Larchmont Avenue. He passed the Larchmont Public Library where there wasn't a single book that could help him and he glanced at the Larchmont Municipal Building meeting rooms where obscure men made public laws as though Larchmont was still a company town of millionaires fleeing the New York summers in the age before air conditioners.

He walked up Larchmont Avenue past the gracious houses in an ingracious age. In the bright sunlight that had burned away the misty morning air Larchmont looked like a sonnet Shakespeare might have written. This Larchmont set in an inland sea, this jewel, this train stop on the Penn Central, this place near the sea where he tried to make a home for himself that would be just a little better than the home his father and mother made for him in Great Neck, this Larchmont where his wife and Shelley might have had a triumphant dinner party together, this Larchmont that pressed on him like a throbbing headache that he could feel building up at the top of his neck, this Larchmont which he would now have to flee like Dracula being hunted by a doctor with a wooden stake. Where would he go to live?

Philip went down Larchmont Avenue, toward the water, the Sound which was now a breathtaking blue. The horizon was already covered with sailing boats. Why didn't he, Elaine, and Michael board the *Sea Islander* and sail deep into the Sound, perhaps to Block Island, Newport. To let the sea wash them clean.

Sunday morning was the Blue Jay race. How easily Michael would have won the Blue Jay race if it had been run last Sunday. Now Philip didn't know what was in Michael's head. Michael had not come to him and he had not gone to Michael. They had all hid from one another in the house. In the Blue Jay race Michael would be out in the open, all eyes on the race, and in the screams and shouts Michael would hear him screaming, "Win, Michael, my God, Michael, win!"

His cries would be heard by Michael racing on the water. The Blue Jay would leap through the waves like a dolphin to win the race for Michael. And that might ease some of the pain that seemed to be etched into Michael's face by that skilled hand of God that can trace on one's face what is in the soul.

Saturday Afternoon

They sat in the Blue Jay as though the low tide had left them stranded on a sandbar.

"What do you think about those people who sail alone around the world?" Amy asked Michael without looking at him. "I think they get into the rhythm of the sea, the days must blend one into the other like margarine. I think they never get lonely. One has to be among people to be lonely." Amy felt if she turned her face to him, Michael would burst into tears.

"I don't think about people who sail alone around the world," Michael said. "There's nothing so special in it. Those people who climb mountains and who sail around the Cape of Good Hope in a twenty-two-foot boat do it to attract attention to themselves and they may be the loneliest people in the world. For what else is there for them to do after they have sailed around the world alone?"

Michael spoke as though all of his words cried out for translation.

"Aren't we supposed to be working on your boat?" Amy asked.

"Yes," Michael said, knowing he couldn't tell Amy.

He dove under the Blue Jay to scrape away the barnacles. The hull had to be swept clean for the race on Sunday. Barnacles slowed the boat. Amy held the Blue Jay upright as he dug into the barnacles that had grown on the boat in just the past week. The barnacles grew in dark clusters clinging like paint. He could only work for thirty seconds at a time, holding his breath, surfacing to fill his lungs, then diving again under the boat and scraping away the barnacles that resisted losing their nesting place. The water was murky. It was low tide. He felt like banging his head against the hull of the Blue Jay. He had watched his father leave the house in the morning and head for Manor Park and had wondered if he should shout at his father from the window and tell him to wait up for him. He had heard his father moving around the kitchen, dropping a bowl that clattered to the floor, as though his father had wanted them to come rushing out of their rooms to help pick up the broken pieces. He never knew silence could vibrate and vibrate.

He would win the Blue Jay race. He would get rid of every barnacle. He and Amy would polish the boat. They would take the Blue Jay out on a trial run. He would win the race if it meant his father might smile at him.

Michael surfaced. He turned his face away from Amy so that Amy wouldn't see what he had been thinking. Amy might guess what had happened because

97

Amy seemed to see into the soul of everyone they knew in Larchmont. Amy baked her own bread. Amy made the best apple pies he ever tasted. Whatever Amy did she did best. In their Latin class she spoke Latin like Larchmont was a suburb of Rome. Amy should crew with him on the Blue Jay. She would make the waves part for them. Michael swam around the Blue Jay to Amy's side and put his arms around her and felt her body against him and wished it had been Amy and not his mother that his father saw.

He knew he couldn't hide his trembling from Amy. He swam under the boat, out of her arms, and came up on the other side, looking at her across the Blue Jay. He turned away as he began to feel her gaze on him. It would do no good for Amy to know, for anyone to know, even his own mind didn't want to know, for it kept looking for a hiding place where his thoughts could be buried like a shipwreck at the bottom of the sea.

"Let's go for a sail," he said.

Amy raised the sails. Michael cast off. In an instant they were out of sight of the Club, the veranda, the land where he felt less at home now than might the thousands of tiny fish that trailed the Blue Jay.

Amy wore a bikini that made her look as naked as a Greek statue. Her body just verged on being a woman's. Even Amy didn't know how magnificent she looked when she undid the top of her bikini as casually as he took off his T-shirt. The sun was overhead. The Blue Jay cut through the choppy water with powerful lunges. Way out they could see the hazy shore of Great Neck where his father had been born, just across the Sound from Larchmont. He must stop thinking of his father or Amy would guess everything or make him tell everything. Amy didn't believe secrets should be hidden, because understanding the secrets was more exciting than hiding the secret. Amy was so much like his mother in the way they both seemed to be listening to you and other voices at the same time, voices he could never hear.

Amy's mother had been in Auschwitz and her father had been a waist gunner in a B-17 Flying Fortress. Maybe that gave Amy a vision he would never have, for to have parents who had seen the devil face to face meant your vision extended beyond the vision of the people he knew in Larchmont, who looked mostly like they couldn't understand people who had missed a meal. Amy never spoke about Auschwitz, nor did her mother, a cheerful woman who made their house on Mayhew Avenue shine like a summer garden.

"My God," Amy said, "what are you thinking about so much? Is it the race? Do you want to win it so bad? Is it the idea of losing? Are you worried about losing? It's just a race. It's actually your first race. Just win and don't worry about losing."

"I want to win," Michael said.

"Why?" Amy asked.

"I think it will make my father happy."

"Won't he be happy even if you don't win?" Amy asked.

"I said I think he will be happy if I win."

"And your mother?"

"Duck!" Michael cried out as the boom swung loose. Michael tacked as they headed for Mamaroneck.

"Does your mother care if you win?" Amy asked. "I don't think she cares who wins or who loses, to quote

Shakespeare. I think of your mother as some kind of a heroine. I can sometimes see her in long dresses sweeping through Washington Square or in a Boston living room quietly putting everyone ill at ease. It's because she always seems to understand what no one else is capable of even imagining. You didn't know your mother and me talked a lot." Amy smiled. "Not about you and me in your bed, but about things that only people in books seem privileged to talk about, like the way ideas come into our minds, the way babies know so much before they can say a single word, how they can communicate almost every idea they need to tell you without saying anything. I don't know why your mother didn't stay in teaching. I would like to have her in class more than some of those teachers we get. Do you like your mother?" Amy asked.

Michael couldn't control the flush that overran his face. He tried to turn his neck back on Amy but he was sure she saw the flush. Amy would be able to trace the flush to its secret place of origin.

"Why did you flush?" Amy asked. "Is it so embarrassing to say you like your mother?"

"I never think of it that way," Michael said. "I don't think of liking or disliking my parents. They are there and I wouldn't know what to do without them or who to see in their place. You remember what we talked about from Descartes? You said he said that of all the things we know best in this world, we know our own existence. And I said, of all the things that we know second best in this world, we know our parents. You laughed. You said parents have a way of behaving as though their children weren't created by them but came to them when they were fifteen or sixteen, all grown up. You said parents didn't seem to have a hand in raising their children, only in keeping them from ever growing up. Well, I don't like to talk about my parents as though I was a full-time job for them. I think they have a life of their own, even if they don't want me to believe it because I may think they are cheating me out of something."

"You said that very well, Michael."

"Thank you," Michael said.

"You haven't tried to touch me in the boat," Amy said. "Why?"

"Do you want me to?"

"Yes."

"Will you move over here?"

Amy moved from the bow of the Blue Jay to Michael. She moved her bare breasts up and down Michael's arm. She could feel Michael trembling in a way she had never felt him tremble before. It wasn't the excitement of her breasts. He had touched her breasts until they were as familiar to him as his own. There was another kind of trembling in Michael, a trembling that begins when vibrations start coming to us that our minds don't understand and it seems we are being bombarded by questions from someone we can never quite identify as ourselves, even though we know it is ourselves asking the questions. This much Amy knew. She didn't want to question Michael. He would tell her when he was ready. There was little they didn't tell each other but they knew how to keep the secrets that mattered. She lay against him, warm, alive, alert, knowing his pulse was racing, and that all he wanted now was to be reassured that his secret was safe. When it came out it would no longer be a secret.

People are made out of funny put-me-togethers and one never knew when they would be handed the next building block in their lives. She kissed Michael's hand and he bravely responded by looking at her directly and letting her see the full anguish he felt, which not even the soft wind blowing on the Sound or Amy's breasts pressing against his legs could keep hidden.

"Do you still see Nancy?" Amy asked, offhand, as though it wasn't a question at all.

"Why do you ask when you know I don't," Michael said.

"I was just wondering what happened to Nancy. I don't see her at school anymore."

"I thought you knew. Her mother's divorce came through. She went to live with her mother in Baltimore."

"I thought she wanted to stay with her father," Amy said. "I remember her saying she never wanted to leave Larchmont. What will she do in Baltimore?"

"Her mother has her seeing a psychiatrist three times a week, and she's going to one of those private schools in Washington, D.C., where everybody wears torn jeans and see-through blouses. She calls me from time to time on the phone because she says she doesn't want to lose contact with the people she grew up with in Larchmont. And she flies up every Sunday morning to see her father and flies back on Monday morning. Nancy says she would like to stay in the plane always and never come down to earth. She says she would like to go to school in Switzerland where they ski all day on the mountains and learn to read menus in three different languages. She talks sometimes like all the world is going past her like water in a stream and she can no more hold the world in her than she could hold a lake in her hands."

"That sounds like Nancy. What else did she say?"

"She says she wishes she was thirty already because she doesn't know how she is going to live until she gets to be thirty. She says she doesn't want to spend her life wandering in and out of the offices of psychiatrists. She says she wishes she could marry someone like her father, but then she might turn on the guy the way her mother tortured her father. She said it is all very confusing being in Baltimore and the only nice thing is driving her car into Washington, D.C., to see the Lincoln Memorial at night. I like the idea of knowing Nancy. She is someone you can talk about without anger."

"You sound like you are making all this up for Nancy," Amy said. Michael swore he saw two blue lights shining in front of Amy and beams of white light coming out of her eyes and a smile on her face that his mother sometimes had, as if she had just swum the Indian Ocean without telling anyone. They both fell into a silence where they didn't dare say any more.

When they came into Larchmont harbor it was near dusk. A chill was in the air. Amy put on her yellow sailing jacket. They moored the Blue Jay and sat for a long time on the boat before they hailed the launch. When it was dark, as though they had been waiting for the dark, they rode to shore watching the lights of the Club. They leapt off the launch just as the music started on the veranda for the Race Week Eve party which they would not go to.

Saturday Night

Elaine stood on the veranda and listened to the orchestra play a fox-trot from the 1920s. It was a trick of the orchestra the club members loved, instant nostalgia. Elaine sipped her Scotch and soda, a drink invented before the 1920s. She had no real friends at the Club. She smiled at Ann Moore who had gained instant fame when she told the rabbi's wife who had been invited to the Club for a luncheon that she would like to read "an unbiased version of the Holocaust." The rabbi's wife said, "Are you sure you know what the Holocaust was?"

From the veranda Elaine admired the solid sailing feel of the Club, just as the Harvard Club on West 44th Street always gave one a solid feel of accomplishment. The Club was like the Hotel Plaza or the Brooklyn Bridge, an institution that had outlived criticism. They had joined the Club to have a place to anchor the *Sea*

Islander. Some of the older members remembered Philip's father as a daring sailor and they would never let Philip forget that his father had rescued a Larchmont sailor who had fallen overboard during the 1957 Bermuda races.

Philip raced the *Sea Islander* under the Club's flag but he never won. Now he wanted Michael to win the Blue Jay race on Sunday. Did Philip hope to please his father who was dead? How strange she found the men in Larchmont. They were so polite, like the elders she remembered from a visit to a Mormon church. The men of Larchmont were anointed boys with their tennis rackets, squash rackets, worn Top-Siders, Lacoste shirts, bulky leather jackets in the winter, Irish swagger hats, their neat tinny smiles; men not daring to grow up to a terror they knew existed, since they read the *Times* every morning—a terror which they hoped they had fled by crossing the border of New York City into Larchmont. The men of Larchmont did nothing but practice success like it was a Canadian Air Force exercise. Philip saw the world could burst apart like a balloon. It had for him, sooner than he'd expected.

They had both agreed to come to the party for Michael's sake, though she knew Michael didn't care. Michael was with Amy and Amy was wiser and bolder than any girl she had ever met. She was good for Michael now and maybe forever. Did Michael confide in Amy? How she would like to know what Amy said.

"Are you going to stay on the veranda with that intense look on your face all night?" Mildred Emerson asked Elaine. "You look like you're going to smash that glass against the wall and declare war on the human race."

"I was just thinking," Elaine said.

"I know you were. But about what? That's what I would like to know." Mildred's son Tom sometimes crewed with Michael. He was a nice boy with a passion to get into Colby College where Philip had some influence. Tom would come over to the house and drink all the ginger ale they had in the refrigerator as though his parents couldn't afford to spend the fifty-five cents a bottle that ginger ale now cost. Tom once told her, "My mother will talk about my father to anybody." She did. Mildred was a psychotherapist, a fact Elaine could never believe, nor did she see how Mildred's patients believed it.

"The men in Larchmont," Elaine said. "These great sailors. Tonight they are going to swim through a sea of gin. Tomorrow morning they will watch their sons race Blue Jays. On Monday they will return to the task of keeping the world afloat. On Friday they will send out for pizza because they don't want their wives to cook. Have I said all this before, I think I have. We are worse than the men. We keep shoving their heads under water when they are drowning."

"I did interrupt something," Mildred said.

"No, it's just the melancholy this place gives me. I think we were born at the wrong time for yacht clubs. This should be a sailing club, nothing else, nothing more, and none of this tinkling music and Japanese lanterns as though F. Scott Fitzgerald had laid out the boundaries of our lives. The generation Fitzgerald wrote about is dead. Fitzgerald wouldn't recognize any of us, would he, with our passion for redeeming coupons for cash at the Grand Union supermarket."

"Did you say you were just on your second Scotch?"

said Mildred, who knew that she and Elaine never exchanged a greater confidence than their knowledge of the weather predictions.

Elaine walked toward the buffet table where she glanced at the food and decided another Scotch and soda would be more appetizing. Had any of the women on the dance floor ever turned to their sons as she had? Probably not. Though Pat Harris once said in their kitchen there was no reason why mothers shouldn't help their sons get over their awe of women by taking them to bed first so they would have a wife when they married and not a body. It was typical of the Friday night talk when they and the Harrises got together to reaffirm themselves, but such talk never became as loose or daring as the talk she remembered in her own kitchen when she was a girl, even if George Harris used to embarrass Pat by saying she gave the best head in Larchmont.

Elaine knew she was just slightly high. It was the only way to get through the night and crawl into her bed alone. Philip would not dare come into their bedroom. He was still frightened of her. They had sat together in the Mercedes as though they expected a bomb to go off when he started the motor. They rode to the Club in silence. They entered the Club in silence. It was crazy of them to come. Where was Philip? She decided it was no accident that Philip had come home early yesterday. It was no accident that he had opened the door to Michael's room just as she began to feel Michael stirring in her, and her own body come alive. She didn't need a fourth Scotch and soda.

She saw Philip with George Harris and Arnold Rosenthal and Frank Wills. They all looked formidable in their blue blazers. They all had sons racing Blue Jays. She waved to them as though she would never see them again and walked out to the veranda. Tomorrow she would watch the race from the veranda. She would yell to Michael. She would cry out his name. She would cheer for him and hope for him to win.

Her neighbors were beginning to stagger past her drunk: the train companions for a half-hour ride of harmless gossip, the tennis partners, the faces she nodded to in the bakery, the faces remembered from lines at the Citibank. The breakdown had come just now, precisely when the orchestra began playing hard rock and the club members began dancing like autistic children striking out in despair to be recognized. They forgot the fox-trot and tinkle of bells. Now they wanted their century to begin. They began dancing to the hard rock with their faces taut and tense, their arms whirling away. Look at us, they seemed to shout to their parents, grandparents, even great-grandparents, who hadn't prepared them for the children they gave birth to, the children they feared. The children they tried to buy off with Nikon cameras, Audis, thousand-dollar wilderness camping trips, Gucci belts worn with patched Levi's. What an extraordinary time it was when parents feared their own children and gave in to their own children as though the children held a pistol at their heads. The parents were the first generation in the history of the world that looked on their children in awe, as though their children possessed a knowledge unobtainable to them, and they slaved after their children to the bewilderment of their children.

Good night Philip, Elaine said, good night Philip. I

won't stay for the end. I'll walk home. It's a warm beautiful night. I don't want to see the end of this party when the roast beef is thrown to the fish. I will walk down these tree-lined streets to our house that now looks like one of those giant turtles turned on its back. I will go up to our room that you have fled. I will hear Michael in his room where he and Amy have probably talked to each other in the language children have that makes them understand one another like two birds in flight. I will hear Michael in his room. I will know he can't sleep. But that is just for now. I will sleep. I am not afraid of sleep. I can sleep if I believe there is more to the world than what I have already seen of it. Good night Philip. Stay with George Harris and Arnold Rosenthal and Frank Wills where it is safer than being with me. But you are still my husband. You and I created Michael out of an embrace that none of us are yet wise enough to understand. Yet we persist.

Elaine walked past the couples on the dance floor, she smiled at Mildred Emerson, who would remember that smile for the rest of her life. Elaine went home to sleep so that she could cheer Michael in the morning from the veranda where he would hear her voice coming on the wind that would fill his sails.

Four

The Sea

The sun was a red glow in the sky. It set the water on fire. The sun burned through the morning fog. It would be a clear and brilliant day. The horizon would be filled with white sails. The spinnaker sails would color the Sound. A slight breeze stirred the curtains. There would be wind for the sails. The winds would not die off in the Sound, trapped by the World Trade towers and the rest of Manhattan's man-made geography that kept the sails slack when one wanted to race before the wind.

Michael saw the curtains move in the breeze. He saw the clear red ball of the sun. He got out of bed to confirm his feeling that it would be a sunny, hot, brilliant day, a perfect day for racing the Blue Jay. At nine o'clock he had to call David Hornig to remind him about the race. By ten they had to be at the Club. At noon the pistol would crack and the Blue Jays would leap forward.

He no longer knew why he had to win the race or whether his parents would even watch the race. He had heard his father climb into the guest room on the third floor. He had heard his mother drinking coffee until three in the morning, which was when he finally fell asleep. He didn't exactly fall asleep. He fell into what Amy called the nightless pit. The bed that swallows you up. The bed that won't let you sleep. The bed that tosses more than a boat in a squall, that must have led to the invention of the flying carpet. The nightless bed carries you downward into a pit that has no bottom. But eventually he fell asleep. It seemed you always fell asleep, no matter how much you tossed, no matter how your legs tingled, no matter how often your head swung from one side of the pillow to the other, as though there was a spot on the pillow that would deliver sleep.

How brilliant Amy was with her dark understanding of things that no one ever talked about. What happened to people like Amy when they became twenty and thirty and fifty? How long could she go on believing she saw things no one else saw? What man could she marry who would live with a woman who could see through to the bottom of his soul as he buttered a piece of toast or shaved himself?

He thought about his sleep, why he had wanted to go to sleep. Wouldn't it have been better to be awake and talk out with himself what had happened? But what talk could erase that tortured look on his father's face, a look of betrayal that he had never seen on any face? People recovered from cancer, open heart surgery, delicate brain surgery. People recovered from seeing hurricanes wipe away their homes, from automobile accidents and seeing someone that they expected to spend the rest of their lives with rammed through the windshield, their heads smashed to pieces. People recovered from seeing bloated, drowned bodies that sometimes washed up on the Sound, bodies that had once been a wife, a sister, a father, a brother. He had seen Mrs. Gertz's body on the beach while her husband sat on the wet sand looking like a piece of seaweed. Mr. Gertz later married a nurse from White Plains Hospital.

When did sleep come? His mother had been drinking coffee all day and until three in the morning. He heard his father use the john three times during the night. At four in the morning he heard the electric clock in the living room, its Westminster chimes that always sounded stately no matter how much the house vibrated. That was it. He must tell Amy. The entire house vibrated through the night. He could feel the wind trying to tear the house from its foundations. But there was no wind during the night. It was a clear, cool night, a full moon, and no wind. The wind didn't come up until he awoke.

He was happy to see it was a real wind, moving from the south. He had no desire to recall the dream that forced him to wake up. Amy was probably the only person on the earth who could interpret the dream anyhow. That was part of his dream, whether to tell Amy what had happened. Amy would be able to explain it all and give it some sense. In the dream he was afraid to tell Amy. No, he didn't dream about Amy. He was only inventing that part of the dream. The real dream had been more horrible. His mother gave birth to a baby and by the time the baby was a child his mother was old and the baby didn't want to have such an old mother and his mother tried telling the baby that she wasn't the mother and the baby kept asking, Then how was I born, how was I born. The baby kept screaming, How was I born, how was I born, how was I made, where did I come from, how can I talk, how can I think, how can I see, I want to go back where I didn't see, didn't talk, didn't think, didn't know there was a me. Take me back there, the baby demanded. Its head started getting bigger and bigger and his mother screamed, No, No, and the baby screamed, You did make me, and his mother screamed, No, No! and the baby said, Take me back, put me back, it's not my time yet. The baby's head was from a different time. "Yes," Amy said, "a million years from now we won't have arms or legs, or stomachs, we will be all heads, all brain, we will need only our brains to explore the universe that we will keep pushing back." So Amy was in the dream. His mother, the baby. Where was his father? Oh, no, Jesus, his father was the baby.

The Race

They were on the veranda. If the women had been wearing long white gowns and straw boating hats and yards of ribbon it could have been the close of the nineteenth century. Instead it was the approach of the end of the twentieth century and the women all wore white slacks and were slightly drunk from the Bloody Marys they had consumed at the long buffet brunch table. The boating men of the nineteenth century had worn blue heavy double-breasted blazers with gold buttons and heavy white flannel trousers even in one-hundred-degree heat. They had never perspired, never complained about the heat, as though surrounded by a halo of breezes from the Atlantic.

In the nineteenth century life in the yacht clubs was ruled by order. The rules were the game. The men who didn't keep the rules were easily found out. The rest of the men took strength from one another and if that failed they always had booze or the women from New York whom they purchased like ballast for their yachts. The boats were big in the nineteenth century. A forty-foot boat was common for the races. The bigger boats soared to sixty, eighty, a hundred feet, and the men on those boats sat and watched the races from deck chairs sipping champagne and stroking the soft responsive thighs of the girls imported from the Broadway theaters for a week on the Sound. The wives in the long white gowns, if they dared, had the student deckhands from Harvard and Yale home for the summer to ride in the saddle. Most of the wives preferred such accommodation to hysteria, which was the common ailment of upper-class women in America in the late 1800s. In the warm balmy evenings the great boats were lit by Japanese lanterns and music would drift from yacht to yacht. The Sound in front of the Club would look like the dreamland it was for the Morgans, the Vanderbilts, the Goulds. Even the water was paved with gold for these Americans. The men were great sailors because the sea was the only mistress they couldn't buy. Once the starting pistol cracked it didn't matter if you were a Vanderbilt, a Morgan, or a Gould, what mattered was how well you understood the wind, the waves, the sails, the boat, and how responsive you could make the boat to your touch. No woman on earth could expect the loving skill these men lavished on their boats to make them win. The great races across the Atlantic, to Bermuda, Block Island, Newport, demanded the concentration of love on the great white sails.

On this Sunday morning the boats in the Sound were smaller. The great hundred-foot racing yachts had disappeared with the nineteenth century. As more men began to sail, the boats got smaller and smaller. The passion to take to the sea boomed after the end of World War II. The size of the boats was all a question of money, of how much money you could put into a boat you would only sail on weekends and perhaps only as far away as the Thimble Islands off the Connecticut shore. Nobody knows how many boats are in the American waters today, but the figure may be ten million, maybe fifteen million, counting everything that sits in the water. On a Saturday morning the Long Island Sound is as crowded as the Long Island Expressway. Even in the winter the frost-biting fleets take off from the Mamaroneck harbor and sail into the freezing water. And it is still the sea that must be mastered. The sea is our mother. We believe this because we all believe we somehow came out of the sea and flopped on the land as living creatures.

All this Michael saw from the Blue Jay as he and David Hornig worked the lines of the boat clean and clear and nosed it into the lineup of Blue Jays that would race around the course of markers. But Michael knew he was racing time, time that would call him to account, a time that Amy called reckoning.

The countdown began.

"Ready?" Michael asked David Hornig.

"Yes," David said, hiking out on the rail.

They both started the ten-second countdown, Michael counting from the stopwatch, both watching for the wisp of smoke from the gun that would send them across the starting line.

Bloody Mary

Philip drank his third Bloody Mary. He asked the bartender on the veranda for half vodka, half tomato juice. Bloody Mary was the drink at the Club this year. It combined booze, tomato juice, and blasphemy. He would not get drunk. He only wanted to see the race through the splendid haze liquor can bring on at eleven in the morning. His back hurt from the bed in the guest room. He was used to the softness of their king-sized bed, the soaring massive pine headboard that had been stripped from a church in New England and turned into a headboard by a crafty dealer on Second Avenue. It was a pumpkin pine, a color he loved because it reminded him of Pilgrim history. He had long ago decided that he was an American. The search for antiques and novelties was the last desperate hope of people who wanted to believe they had a heritage worth saving. He remembered a Sunday flea market held on Harbor Island where the sailing boats anchored and the people from Mamaroneck swam into the foul water. He saw a table of old glass, pots, vases, and two women selling stuff emptied from Larchmont homes. A man in a blue nylon jacket picked up a metal strainer with three hooks on the bottom and a wire chain that looked like an instrument for scooping up lobsters. The man hesitated. He put down the pot. A woman in a green dress picked up the pot. It was marked two dollars. She said, I'll pay one-fifty. The Rotary lady said, All right. The man in the blue nylon jacket saw the pot disappear from his grasp. He heard the Rotary lady tell the woman buyer, "That was used by the coal miners in Pennsylvania to carry lunch. A rope would be let down in the mine and they would hook this basket onto the rope and their lunch would be let down to the miners. The hooks on the bottom held their jackets. You bought a piece of history." The man in the nylon jacket almost burst into tears. Something had slipped out of his grasp, his life, never to return. How instantly his body showed despair. How swiftly the muscles throughout his body, the coloring on his skin, the position of his eyes, his mouth, his hands, showed despair. It had slipped away. He would never again see another Pennsylvania miner's lunch basket.

It is slipping away, Philip told himself, it is slipping away. My life is slipping away. He could have been tied to a mast in a boat floundering in the Atlantic. The Bloody Mary would not bring him to shore. He sipped on the Bloody Mary. How beautiful the Sound looked. The boats looked painted on the sky. He would like to go on one of those year-long voyages that ladies who inherit a fortune take as soon as their husbands are laid in their graves. Forty-seven ports, around the world, all those millions of people in the forty-seven ports, those lives he would never penetrate except through the travel section of the Sunday *Times*. In Hong Kong the tortured look on his face would soften as he dined on fried eel and saffron rice and girls served him with bells on their ankles.

He put down his Bloody Mary. Elaine was on the far end of the veranda. She looked out on the Sound. Occasionally she would glance in his direction. He could not interpret the look on her face, there was no indication that she wanted him to join her to watch the race. She too sipped on a Bloody Mary. She said hello to Esther Furnas who once sang in a Broadway show and now sold Givenchy scarves at Bergdorf Goodman. They spoke for a minute and then Esther Furnas wandered off with a drink in her hand. He could barely distinguish the other faces on the veranda. They had the eager look of parents who want their sons to win. They were all waiting for the gun to go off, the race to start, the winner to be their son.

Was Michael his son forever? Or would Michael slip out of his grasp like the Pennsylvania coal miner's lunch pail? If he and Elaine divorced would Michael still be his son? In the Larchmont churches this morning, was the eating of the wafer the son eating his father? In some long-forgotten tribes the sons ate their father. They fought their father the king for their mother the queen. In some forgotten tribes the sons had to marry the queen mother when the father died. In some tribes two and three sons were married to their mother. But this wasn't some tribe waiting for

Margaret Mead to show up. This was Larchmont and he was on the veranda finishing his fourth Bloody Mary and looking across the veranda at a woman who would draw the wrath of everyone on the veranda if he started to broadcast what she had done. Would they really care? How foreign all these people were to him, these people who showed no emotion except when one of their children was drowning offshore and then they screamed for help like other mortals.

The Club blended everyone into a hazy Bloody Mary. One of the sons would win. He wanted Michael to win. Maybe there was some way of erasing Friday afternoon. Now he was getting drunk. He could not start an argument with Elaine. He could not walk over to her. He must not speak to her. He must not wonder if he would ever be in bed with her again. They were both slipping away. It was like that movie where Tyrone Power was the leader on a lifeboat and he decided who should live and who should die and the people he saved on the lifeboat hated him for forcing them to see how close they were to death, how little choice they had if Tyrone Power decided they should be the ones flung off the lifeboat. Elaine and Michael were slipping away. That was a possibility that he now felt like the wind that had slipped up on him and chilled the back of his neck. There was a possibility they would never again live like a family. Who would get the leather couch in the living room that had been shipped from London? How would they divide the paintings, the chairs? Who would get the beach towels, the Hermes towels that Elaine had bought for forty-five dollars a towel at Bonwit Teller, that repaid themselves a thousand times when conversation went dead in the living room? Who would be left with the worst memories? Would they ever see one another again as they once were?

He found himself walking over to Elaine's side of the veranda. He was now standing behind her. Elaine didn't turn to greet him. She knew he was standing behind her. She brought up her Bloody Mary to sip on and he felt an uncontrollable urge to force her to bite into the glass, to slam her mouth down on the glass, to hear her scream. Instead, he said, "Do you think Michael will win?" The starting gun went off.

Elaine

Elaine wore a white boating hat, white slacks and a blue blazer from Abercrombie & Fitch that Michael had outgrown. She had decided to dress the part after facing an empty breakfast table. Michael was gone, leaving half a glass of orange juice. Philip couldn't break his habit and the crumbs from his toasted English muffin were on the counter.

During the night she had carried on a dialogue with an emissary from another planet whom she couldn't identify but who seemed to know all about her. Just before dawn she decided that the emissary was her cousin Brewster who had walked down the gangplank of the *Mayflower* and who promptly had sex with the first Indian woman he could find. He had heard in London that the Indians were savages, although the Indians who had turned up at Windsor Castle had seemed to act like Dutch diamond merchants. He wrote in his diary that he was disappointed in the Indian woman and said perhaps he should have beaten her first.

Elaine couldn't remember a notable American man who had been proud of his wife. Lincoln suffered Mary. Roosevelt suffered Eleanor. Nixon turned his Pat into a tinseled doll and thought he could cleanse himself by not sleeping with her. The wife of Henry Adams swallowed poison and she is not even a ghost in his incredible autobiography. Jefferson had his black woman. Kennedy his Las Vegas show girls. What American marriages could the *Encyclopaedia Britannica* index with pride? Fitzgerald and Zelda were a traveling horror show. Willa Cather was smart, she never married. What a different America there would be if American men and women had started out as pioneers in marriage forgetting the bad habits of Europe. She had said this to her cousin Brewster. He had laughed, and just before he disappeared he told her that she was absolutely right and that on other planets men and women were learning to live together. "What planets?" she remembered asking desperately just as the garbage men woke her with the rattling of cans.

She had lain in bed aware that she was alone. The position of her body startled her. She was spread-eagled. Her legs flung out, her arms flung out, her body naked. It took her an hour to awake from her nighttime voyage. Philip and Michael were in their own beds and she couldn't begin to guess what kind of a voyage they were on. Michael would never tell her and Philip wouldn't dare. Three people sleeping in three different beds in the same house who had once all slept together. Michael in her for nine months,

Philip for all the years of their marriage. Going into Michael's room had been the continuation of a dream that seemed to extend back to the beginning of time. At first it frightened her, living so deep in the past, because she now knew dreams were the real history, not only of her past, but of all experiences that enabled people to get through the extraordinary event of being born. Michael had been in her bed, in her arms, a hundred times before she knocked on his door Friday and changed the history of their family.

Elaine sipped on her third Bloody Mary of the morning. She had never been able to get drunk when she wanted to be drunk. She envied the Larchmont ladies who did get drunk. They managed to be free and loose and they would remember their beginnings in Brooklyn or the Bronx or Minnesota. They were less tragic when they were drunk. They were even pleasant. They talked freely about their husbands, as though they were an act at Lincoln Center.

Elaine put her drink down on one of the tiled wrought-iron tables scattered over the veranda. Michael and David Hornig were busy in the Blue Jay. Once she thought Michael looked up and recognized her on the veranda and waved his hand. Michael had a race to win. She didn't know a single person on earth with whom she could discuss Friday afternoon. She would not go to a psychiatrist. She would have to live this one out alone. She couldn't convince Philip of anything but the righteousness of his anger. She could see he was frightened of a divorce, the inevitable separation, the loss of her, for he did feel he had laid claim to her over the years even if there weren't many days between them when they really possessed one another. She always figured those days would come later when they could no longer avoid each other. But now those days might never come. That was a terrible loss for both of them. She shook in the cool breeze. Her hands were wet. The back of her neck was cold. She tied her Hermes scarf around the collar of her blue jacket. How she longed for it to be a year from now.

The Blue Jays were nosing up to the starting line. The Sound was the way she liked to see it, a long line of white sails. The water a dark blue. The sea gulls diving for food. The sun bright even as she felt chilled. How she would like to be in the Blue Jay with Michael. They had a race to win, she and Michael. She would never let Michael work Friday out for himself, even if he had his cool friends to go to who knew about divorces in their families, screams of anger, suicide attempts. Win Michael! she heard herself saying. Win Michael! Win! Win! My God, what lies ahead of you? To win not just the race, that's nothing, but to win yourself, as I have not done yet for myself, or your father, if he ever would. Philip would die like the men she read about in the *Mamaroneck Daily Times,* a sudden massive heart attack, the startled look in his eyes that life was over.

She felt Philip behind her. She shivered and the pit of her stomach went cold. She quickly finished the last of the Bloody Mary before she turned to face him. He was still wearing that terrible look of betrayal. The starting gun went off and the Blue Jays leapt forward.

The Blue Jay

The Blue Jay leapt forward as the gun cracked and cheers rose from the veranda. Michael felt the wind at his back. He didn't see the other Blue Jays in the race. He only saw the open water before him, the invisible line ahead that he was about to cross. The boat responded magically to his touch. He was in the lead as the gun broke the long silence. He would hold the lead. He would keep the wind for himself. The sails flared out. The water was choppy but it didn't hold back the boat. He had scraped the bottom of barnacles. The hull was swift and clean. He wished Amy was crewing with him. Amy had a way of talking to the wind. She spoke to the sails, to the waves. Amy crewed on his boat like she was an ancient figurehead carved on the bow, a goddess of the sea. She had showed him a will she had written where she said that she wanted to be buried at the bottom of the sea. Not ashes to ashes, dust to dust, Amy had said, but back to the sea where every form of life is experimented with and shapes exist that man has never seen. Amy had sailed since she was five. "The sea is there to be conquered," she told him as they lay in her bed, her hot body on top of his, leaving them both like a boat in a calm.

The first marker was ahead. He was twenty feet in the lead of the nearest boat. He was almost hanging over the water, his feet gripping the stirrups. He brought the Blue Jay about and swept toward the second marker. The wind was good to him. The sails were full. There would be no slack this afternoon. He only had to stay in the lead to win. Amy spoke to boats as she spoke to the trees in Manor Park, or the big rocks that remained from the second glacier. Sometimes he thought Amy was born in some fireball that fell during the August moon. In bed Amy had said to him, "Don't ever worry about your father and mother, they have to make it on their own. They have had you all of their lives. That kind of love goes on forever, but it doesn't mean you have to feel yourself locked into your mother and father forever. Most fathers and mothers want it that way because they think they love their children in a way they have loved no one else, not even themselves, but that isn't true. Real love is when you can let go, when you dare to let go, when you don't feel threatened like my father who turns white in the face when he hears my mother say that she is going to a movie by herself or with a friend. My father immediately thinks my mother is deserting him. What a tortured man he must be."

Amy was on the bow of the Blue Jay, carved by a Baltimore woodcutter, painted in brilliant reds and greens, ready to take fifty-foot waves, smiling at the whales sunning themselves in the Indian Ocean. The second marker was passed. He swung the boat down the last leg of the course, heading toward the mid-leg buoy marked with a red flag. He saw the Club pennant flying in the wind. The sky was waving hands.

He was sailing into port. He had crossed the Atlantic in a wild storm. Hundred-foot waves swamped his boat. He was making landfall. There were the houses on the shore, the windows shining in the sun. There were the hills, the Manor houses, people waving from the shore, the sails billowing in the wind. The Blue Jay rolled and rose in the water and drove toward the shore. Landfall. He would be home. Get ready to lower the anchor. There was the harbor! There was land after a sleepless night. There was the shore. He could see his house. He could see his room. He could see into his room. He could see his bed. He could see his father's face with its look of betrayal. Michael had taken that look to bed with him Friday night. At one in the morning he had called Amy. He knew Amy didn't get to sleep until two or three in the morning. She had her own phone in her room. She picked up on the first ring.

"Are you asleep?"

"You know I'm not asleep."

"I'm not asleep."

"Why? Can't you sleep?"

"I can't tell you now."

"Then tell me at the Club this afternoon."

"I want to tell you, but I can't."

"You sound like you are screaming," Amy said.

"Am I screaming?"

"I just said you sound like you are screaming."

"I was screaming. But nothing came out. Can you scream with nothing coming out?"

"Yes," Amy said.

"Do you have trouble falling to sleep?"

"No."

"I do."

"I know. Do you still feel like racing Sunday?"

"Yes," he said. But he wasn't sure.

"Then race. And win," Amy said. "Win!" And she hung up.

A Blue Jay was at his side. It was Tom Russell from Elm Avenue. He was gaining on Michael. They were side by side. Michael was heading into Tom Russell's boat. Tom was yelling at Michael to get out of the way. Michael could see him heading for the final buoy before the finish. He jibbed his boat into a close line for the buoy. He had to cut Tom Russell off. Tom Russell wouldn't dare fight him at the buoy. He would give way. He wouldn't fight to win. He would hold his boat back. Michael knew he would. The buoy rose up in front of him. He was going to crash into it. He was going to hit the marker, and that would be the end of the race. "Win," Amy had said. That was something he had to do. "Win!" He missed the marker. The red flag whipped across his bow. Tom Russell was into a wide swing. His boat was way off. The race would be over in minutes. Michael had only to stay on course. The wind had to keep up its pace, but no other boat was in sight. He could hear the yelling from the veranda. He could see the hands waving in the air. There were Bloody Marys on the veranda. His mother and father were waving their Bloody Mary glasses. They were all at the edge of the veranda. What a great, glorious picture they all made cheering their sons. What a glorious victory I have won, he thought. I lost my mother. I lost my father.

Amy

I would like to marry Michael in a few years. I think we understand each other. The new marriages will have to happen through understanding, not love. I don't know anyone in the books I've read who was truly in love. The lovers in the books were all desperate for recognition. They seemed to need a second person to tell them they were alive, to make them feel alive. Instead of feeling alive, they were always tortured. For if the love ended, then they would come to an end. Love was invented to keep people in torment. I see it in Larchmont. People need to understand one another more than they need to love one another. I heard my mother tell my father this in the only burst of real passion I ever saw in her. How great she looked, her eyes blazing, her body on fire, her voice trembling with a truth that she knew to be true. This is supposed to happen in sex but sex has become more polluted than the rivers that flow past the manufacturing towns.

Michael wanted to tell me what he knew last night

while everybody else was celebrating the races, but he was afraid. I could feel the vibrations of fear from his body. The vibrations formed a wall around his body. They were so intense that I could almost feel and touch them. I didn't try to force Michael to tell me what he desperately wanted to tell me. Instead I said, "Let's go out for a walk by the Sound." It was ten o'clock at night. Michael said, "Should we take out the boat?" I said, "No, let's just walk."

Walking is something most people don't do any-more. Real walking is feeling your feet on the earth and knowing you are performing a remarkable act, walking on two legs while most of the rest of the ani-mal kingdom is on four legs. How often I wonder what the animals think of me. We have two dogs in the house. Freddie and Alex understand every word said to them and they talk with their eyes and their tails in a way that is so accurate, so true, that I wonder if humans weren't led astray by developing language. Our language tells us nothing. We express ourselves so much better by our vibrations, our bodies, our hands, shoulders, the way we transform our bodies into grief, sadness, statues that even Michelangelo could only copy, for sculpture tells us again what we are capable of expressing with our bodies.

Michael looked as though Michelangelo had carved him out of hamburger patties. Michael won the Blue Jay race but it seemed to give him no pleasure. He held the trophy cup as though it was filled with his tears. Michael whispered to me on the veranda, "I must see you tonight." He spoke as though he was a messenger bringing me terrible news.

Michael will be forty in the year 2000. I will be

thirty-nine. I don't believe there will be anything over-whelming in the year 2000. The year 1900 passed with only fireworks and a sense that life was speeding up to a dreary end. At least this is what Mr. Simpson said in American History with an air of being above "all that." I mentioned this to Michael and Michael said, "In the year 2000 we will just be older, not wiser."

We walked toward Manor Park, past half-lit houses trying to save on electricity—my father screams every time the bill goes over a hundred dollars a month. We walked along the path until we came to the rocks over-looking the Sound. I love the water. There, I used the word love. Don't you see, the water doesn't have to love me back! I love the water. The water doesn't have to love me back. I love Nathaniel Hawthorne. Nathaniel Hawthorne doesn't have to love me back. I love the old Greta Garbo movies. Greta Garbo doesn't know I am alive. I do not love Michael. I will never love Michael. I do not want to love Michael. I want Michael to see me one day as clearly as he sees problems in math. I do not want to be a mystery to Michael.

We climbed up on the rocks and sat for a long time without speaking. The boats swayed at anchor. We could have been in Greece or Cannes or the Bay of Naples. The water makes all places where people live look eternal. Michael wanted me to ask him why a blue flame was vibrating all around his body, but I didn't. There are some people who can see into the soul of another person. I am not one of them. I do not believe that people have souls. I believe the earth has a soul, the world, all of life, there is a soul to the world, but not to individual people. We aren't developed yet enough to have a soul. A soul is overwhelming. It flows into everything alive. People do not flow into one another. People hide from one another. Michael is trying to hide from me. He wants desperately to tell me a secret but the words can't form themselves out of him, the words refuse to surface from inside of Michael. I will be patient with him. It is not good to force secrets from people. Then they feel ashamed. One must wait until the secret has exhausted itself. There are no secrets that we know.

Michael said, "Do you remember us talking about those people who sail from the coast of England in a sixteen-foot boat to go around the world. I wonder what it is like to be a person who sets out alone to sail around the world."

"My father would say commuting into Manhattan every day is harder."

"And the sailor would say, sailing around the world is easier."

"Are you telling me that you want to sail from Larchmont to Asia and back again?"

"I can see them standing on the veranda cheering me as my boat comes into Larchmont harbor after an eighteen-month voyage. The crazy TV news reporters asking me how it felt to be alone, or was I frightened. Those reporters aren't real."

"They don't get paid to be real."

"We're going on a sail," Michael told me, as though I had been in on his plans from the start.

"Who?" I asked. Now the secret was beginning to work its way loose.

"My family."

"Oh," I said. I wasn't in on the plan. "What is this sail?"

"My father announced it at dinner tonight. He said we were going to take the *Sea Islander* and sail to Block Island."

"Is he a good enough sailor?"

"Between the three of us I think we can make it."

"Sailing to Block Island can be dangerous."

"I know."

"Did you ever do it before?" I asked.

"No. Once we started for Block Island and a storm came up off New Haven. The storm lasted all day and we changed our plans."

"I like Block Island," I said. "It can be a very moody place. Did you ever climb down Mohegan's Bluff? That's where you get the feel of the Atlantic. The old ships used to crash right into the cliffs. Are you going to sail all night, or are you going to anchor?"

"The plan now is to sail all night."

"Then you need watches for lobster pots, good charts, and luck. I didn't know your father was so daring."

"He isn't," Michael said.

"Then it can be a very dangerous sail," I said.

"There's a problem in our family," Michael said, not looking at me but at the water, as though the water wasn't listening. "I can't tell you about the problem because I don't really understand it yet. I want to know more about it before I tell you. My father thinks that if the three of us take a five-day sail to Block Island we can talk more freely on the boat. We'll be all by ourselves. We'll have a lot of time to talk unless a storm comes up. My father says there are too many distractions in the house. The telephone rings. Somebody is always going to the refrigerator. The record player or the TV is going. Somebody stops by. The car needs gasoline. He says the sail will be right."

"It sounds damn right to me," I said. "When do you leave?"

"Tomorrow morning."

"Which means you'll be back next weekend. I'll be walking up and down the Larchmont shoreline looking for you. You're not worried about the sail, are you?"

"You know that I am."

"Do you want to tell me what your father wants to talk about on the sail?"

"I wish I knew," Michael said. "I wish I could guess. I don't know, Amy. I can't imagine. It'll be like sailing into a sea without charts or compass, and with a mast that will crack at the first heavy wind. People need charts, just like sailors need charts. I don't think my father has a chart for this sail. My mother just might."

Michael said no more about the sail. This morning I went to the Larchmont harbor and waved him good-bye. I stayed until the *Sea Islander* was out of sight. Departure and landfall. Departure is when a ship moves off from its mooring and heads toward a point of land. Landfall is the sighting of land. In between there is the sea.

Five

The Whirlwind

I cannot leave those three people alone on a thirty-one-foot boat in a measureless sea to let them work out their problems. It is not fair to them. They need all the help they can get. Even if my own help is questionable, I have to offer it. In the end they may turn out to be smarter and braver than any of us. They are sailing into unmeasured waters. Just as children experience more than they have language to describe, so it is with adults. For adults are little more than grown children at this stage of world history. I don't say this to be wise. It is the unmistakable observation of those who have taken the time to look at the activities of men and women. Children dominate the world. It is time we moved on. We cannot forever believe that our lives must be forever dominated by what we were or were not as children.

Here my sympathies are with Elaine. She believes that we are trying to recapture our past and the more the past eludes us, the more we suffer. In some way or other, Elaine will have to make this clear to her husband, a man who believes it is not right for him to be bewildered. Michael believes the myth of his generation, that he is somehow in possession of knowledge that is more exact, more true, than anything his parents have ever known. This would be nice if it were true. We are a long way from the day when men will be secure in what they know. Today we still worship more gods than did the Greeks. Every person caught in the grip of a personal vision of himself worships a stranger god than the natives who build models of airplanes in the trees and then wait for the god of the airplane to return to them. When the vision narrows down to oneself and nothing else can be seen of the wide world, we are fooled. It is not good to be alone. Men have known this from the beginning of time. Men have endured every kind of evil not to be alone.

Amy spoke beautifully about departure and landfall. This is the way all voyages begin and end if they don't suffer disaster.

The *Sea Islander* is under full sail. A steady wind is carrying her along the Connecticut shore. Long Island Sound is still full of boats and sails but soon the pleasure boats will be heading back to their moorings and the Sound will be an endless sea. This is when we must all come aboard and give what help we can. It is a voyage we must all make sooner or later. It is a voyage we often make in our sleep when we dream, as we try to remember a golden vision of the past. There's the boat! Look at the sails in the wind! Look at the bow plunging into the water! Elaine is at the tiller and she is steering by the compass, holding the *Sea Islander* steady for Block Island.

Michael's Log

We started taking supplies aboard at 8:30 A.M. I think we cleaned out the Grand Union. We're going on a five-day sail but we have enough food to take us to the Azores. Most of the food is in cans. Dad said we shouldn't waste a lot of time with cooking. Tuna fish will be our staple. We all worked carrying the supplies aboard. Mom even smiled, something she hasn't done in days. I get funny vibrations about Dad. This trip was his idea and I keep getting the vibration that he thinks something important will happen on the voyage. He acts a little like Gregory Peck in that terrible movie of *Moby Dick* they show sometimes on TV. If Mom is Dad's Moby Dick he is never going to harpoon her. Mom is too elusive. Besides, the *Pequod* went down smashed to pieces by Moby Dick. I wish Amy had joined us on this trip. But Dad said no guests. He said it like a captain sailing under sealed orders. Dad doesn't know what kind of voyages Amy has made into the human spirit. Just last night Amy said she went again on that trip back again into her mother's womb. It gets easier and easier to go back, Amy told me. Amy said she doesn't like to go back now, but there is no stopping it once it begins. Amy said this time she could feel her father forcing his way into her mother and she felt his dick plunging into her mother and it was getting close to her and she felt her father was trying to drive his way past her mother and into her. "It was terrible," Amy said, "like he had to touch me with his dick, to feel that I was there and that he had a part in my making. He must have excited my mother, because she began heaving her hips up in the air and I thought I was going to be torn apart between the two of them. I think this is what we want in fucking, to touch one another in that spot where we think life has a beginning." I can't imagine what Amy will be like when she is a full-grown woman. Men will flee from her like they do before a dam that has broken.

I still don't know why I lack the courage to tell Amy what happened between me and Mom. Maybe I feel Amy is too wise and what she will tell me will haunt me forever. Words can stick in the mind. Dad said this voyage will make us a family or else we will go our separate ways like people who meet on a train and then get into different taxicabs at Union Station in Chicago. Dad is always making references to Chicago. There is something about Chicago that fascinates him. He says one of the biggest thrills of his life was to walk down North Michigan Avenue and feel the fog close over him. When Dad goes to Chicago he stays with a friend who has an apartment on the eighty-fifth floor.

Dad says it is like magic to sit in the living room and see the fog approach the windows, to see the rain, the clouds. Amy is right. We are all poets. Mom looks at Dad in an admiring way when he talks about Chicago as though all he needed was a beard to be a poet. But Mom would have never married a poet. We would move to Chicago, Dad says, if I could figure out a way of making a living in Chicago. It is an American city, Dad says, as though he wants a hold on a tradition that escapes us in Larchmont. There are no traditions in Larchmont, if one excludes the Bloody Marys at the Club, Dad says. He says he is leaving no memory behind him, no one to remember him, which isn't altogether true. I think he stays with Mom because he has invested so many of his years with her, but now he wears that terrible look of betrayal which maybe the sea will wash away.

We set sail at 9:30 A.M., loaded to the gunnels. There was a strong wind out of Larchmont. The *Sea Islander* has a different touch and feel than the Blue Jay. It was as though the boat knew we were going on a long voyage. All the other boats under sail looked like toys on the water. We were moving on a course set for Norwalk. From Norwalk we would enter the expanse of the Sound.

Mom was unusually silent when we took the supplies aboard. When we cast off she was at the tiller. She kept her eyes straight ahead, making a swift departure from the shore. She didn't look back. She looked as though we were sailing away forever from our house in Larchmont.

Dad didn't talk either. He sat in the galley studying the charts. We plan to sail all night, but that may be a problem if the water gets rough. The weather reports say nothing about strong winds, but at this time of year anything can happen on the Sound and the wind shifts are sudden. Two of us will have to stay awake if we sail all night. Dad said we will make that decision when we approach the Thimble Islands, which is almost midway to Block Island.

When we got to Norwalk Dad took over the tiller. He said the water traffic was too hard for Mom to handle. The Sound was filled with boats. The motorboats like to scare the hell out of you by thundering down on your bow and crossing with inches to spare. It is the only thrill open to the men who drive the powerboats like trailer trucks and who can't take the indifference of the sea. The sea doesn't care how fast you go. There are no races to win. The water is endless. Dad knows this. Dad is good in the sailboat. He is busy every minute, always checking the sails, the lines. He is always tying lines down. Dad says there shouldn't be any surprises on a boat. Dad says you should always be ready for what the sea throws at you. This takes constant attention, constant work. The lines can never be tangled. Dad says if the boom hits you in the head you have to remember it is traveling at the speed of a freight train. How different Dad acts on land. On land Dad seems to feel he isn't prepared for anything that happens, life is always a surprise. I guess it is.

We are all too alert. Too tense. I could see Mom's hand turn white on the tiller.

At 11 A.M. I made tea for all of us. Mom's hand shivered when I handed her the tea. Dad took his tea to the bow of the boat. Just as we approached Norwalk,

Dad yelled out, "Boat ahead, boat ahead!" It looked as though Mom was driving down on a boat crossing our bow. We missed the boat by inches. I decided I would spend my time keeping a sharp lookout for boats, lobster traps, rocks, buoys, floating logs, and Mom.

When we sailed past the old beat-up lighthouse in the Norwalk harbor, the one that looks like a real monument, Mom spoke for the first time since we set out. "Why didn't somebody in Norwalk think of giving it a coat of paint for the Bicentennial," she said as Dad joined us at the tiller. Dad wore a silk scarf that he had tied around his head like a pirate, blue denim shorts, a Lacoste shirt, and his Top-Siders.

"I think we may tie up at the Thimble Islands for the night," Dad said. "The sky doesn't look too good. We may run into rain or a squall during the night. I think it will be better to tie up at the Thimbles. It's a good harbor but we have to get there before dark. The rocks are dangerous at the entrance to the harbor there. It's hard enough getting into the Thimbles during the daylight."

Dad didn't look at Mom when he spoke. "All right," she said, in a voice that said the real voyage hadn't begun yet. "I like the Thimbles. It's a little like the Maine coast. I like those pretty houses with the oil lamps in the windows and those old men smoking pipes, always looking up at the sky."

"It's the Thimbles then," Dad said. He hadn't listened to what Mom said.

It was 2:30 P.M. when we set a course for the Thimble Islands. We will anchor there for the night and sail in the morning for Block Island.

I am still learning about boats. Dad has said you can't live in Larchmont without a boat. When we first bought the Blue Jay Dad gave Mom lessons in Mamaroneck. Mom took to sailing right away. I started right out with Mom, and Dad let me take the tiller when I was ten. I had permission to take the boat out alone after I showed Dad I could rig the Blue Jay and get it under way without any trouble. But none of us knew much about charts except Dad or navigating at night or currents or any of the secrets of sailing that come to you after years on the water. Occasionally we would take the boat across the Sound to the Long Island side, but that was sailing almost in a straight line with hundreds of boats in the water all around you. I must admit to a certain fear of the water. Alexander Brenner took a Blue Jay out one Saturday and he was never seen again. His boat was found floundering near New Rochelle. They searched for days for Alex's body but it never floated to the surface. He vanished as though he had never existed. We had a memorial service for him at school. I remember crying, the tears streaming down my face because I liked Alex and we used to sail together and I could not imagine him eaten by the fish in the Long Island Sound. Sharks sometimes swim into the Sound and Alex may have been eaten by a shark because bodies almost always surface after a drowning. Nobody could figure out how Alex disappeared from the boat and there was some talk that he may have deliberately drowned himself. Amy didn't think so. Amy said Alex didn't duck soon enough and the boom hit him in the head and he went overboard.

Elaine's Log

We put into the Thimble Islands at sunset. Philip and Michael guided the boat past the massive rocks, some hidden, most rising out of the water. The Thimble Islands are like a Maine shore transplanted to Connecticut. The entrance to the harbor is treacherous at evening. The wind was with us. An old man in an outboard motorboat wearing a baseball cap came up and welcomed us to the harbor. He said it was a safe harbor. How little he knows. There are no more safe harbors. How often I have envied the people living in the Thimble Islands in those lovely houses perched on the rocks with their kerosene lamps going into the evening. They are the kind of people that you feel live forever. The wives look comfortable like deep down quilts, the men like retired sea captains. None of it is true. The men commute to New Haven or New

York and they probably drink more martinis than they consume kerosene in their antique lamps bought at garage sales.

We sailed past the mouth of one harbor that looked congested and dropped anchor in a harbor facing the open Sound. We were in a channel with houses on either side of us. One island had only one house. How grand it looked. Ahead of us we saw a platform that looked like the beginning of a Greek temple. It was the foundation of a house that never got built. Most people are the servants of the houses they own. The sky was a great burst of joy. Magnificent bursts of color stretched across the entire sky—yellows, green, blue, purple—all coming from the sun, a red ball in the sky, giving us life from 93 million miles away, which should tell us something else about ourselves that we can't comprehend. One day I will make up a list of the things we understand and the things that are a complete mystery. It will be interesting to see how much of our lives is hidden from us. I am bored by American poets who wear beards. Where are the clean-shaven giants? What a surprise it will be to women when they realize they have no secrets to tell.

Michael and Philip secured the *Sea Islander.* I went into the galley to prepare drinks. A vodka martini for Philip, a Pepsi-Cola for Michael, a gin and tonic for myself. I prepared a plate of cheddar cheese, Ritz crackers, and slices of hot pepperoni that we bought on Chatsworth Avenue.

Philip said, "Do you want to take the small boat and row ashore?" It was the first time we had spoken in hours.

"No," I said. "What would we do on shore?"

"I guess nothing. There is a town nearby that you can get to by a motorboat that operates like a taxi service."

"What would we do in town?" I asked. "I thought we were sailing away from towns."

"Then we'll stay on the boat and start up again about eight. That should bring us into Block Island sometime in the late afternoon."

"If there's no fog," Michael said. "Block Island can be completely hidden by fog. The Russells sailed right past Block Island into the open Atlantic. They were spotted by a freighter. If it wasn't for the freighter they would have been in trouble."

"Block Island is famous for its wrecks," Philip said. "The shore used to be lined with wrecks of old boats. We won't get lost. If we do run into a heavy fog we'll sit out the fog. We'll be hearing the ferryboat that comes from New London. But with this kind of sunset I don't think we're going to run into fog."

How I admire the sun. The sunset lingered, the way I like to linger in front of a mirror. When the sun was gone, the air became damp. I put on my fisherman's sweater. If left below, the sweater would soak up the dampness. But on my body the sweater was warm and kept away the dampness. Michael put on a foul-weather jacket. Philip put on the Danish sweater I bought him at Saks which he likes because it is stretched out of shape and gives him a casual air. The *Sea Islander* rocked gently in the water. There was no pull on the anchor. There was no chance of a storm sweeping in from the Sound. I went into the galley to prepare dinner. Philip was into his third vodka martini. Michael remained on deck. He was fascinated by the kerosene lamps flickering in the windows offshore.

Philip watched me light the stove. He sipped on his vodka martini. He didn't offer to help me at the stove. He didn't speak. He studied me. He stared at my breasts. I could see him studying my legs. It was as though he was looking for a sign of the devil's growth on me. I suppose I should have stripped off my clothes to let him study me in the galley under the low-wattage lights that flickered almost as gracefully as the kerosene lamps. I knew he was aroused, but he didn't dare make a move toward my body to do what he always likes to do, slip his hands under my sweater and play with my breasts until the nipples stand out. He likes to roll the palm of his hand on my nipples, enjoying the weight of my breasts, cupping my breasts under the sweater, which I also like. Now he sat and stared at me and I pretended not to notice, busy with the chopped sirloin that would be our first dinner at sea.

I suppose it made no difference that his son had been in me for nine months and that his son had come out through my vagina, all that we have a way of forgetting. Philip saw me glance at the table where he was sitting in the galley. Once when we were off East Hampton he stretched me out on the seat alongside the kitchen table top and lifted up my legs and entered me as the boat rocked in the water.

The kitchen table in the galley folds down into a double bed, but we will not be sleeping together. The sleeping arrangements were settled when we stored our gear. Michael noticed that we would each have our own berth.

I rang the ship's bell for dinner. We sat down to a

solemn dinner, almost as though we were the original Pilgrims starting out from Plymouth for the new world.

My last entry in the ship's log took place at 10 P.M.

I went out of the galley onto the deck. I walked to the bow. The sky was clear and bright. The stars shone as though they had been painted in the sky by a third grader. I wrapped myself up in a British convoy coat. I lay on my back on the deck and looked up into the full sky. I let myself be carried into the vastness of the sky. I could leap from star to star. I roamed from planet to planet. On Jupiter I sang nursery rhymes I had forgotten from my childhood. On Mars I thought I recognized the terrain as Arizona. When I came down to earth I saw Philip peeing off the deck of the boat. The moonlight caught his penis. It shone. His flaccid penis suddenly became erect. Erect it seemed as much a part of the sky as the moon which still kept its secrets from us. Philip peed in a wide arc off the boat. When he finished he held on to his penis, reluctant to put it away. I had a psychology professor who told our astonished class that if men were aware of all the complicated mechanisms that had to work just right for them to have an erection, they would probably never be able to have an erection. The vagina can stretch to take any size penis. The penis must be erect to enter the vagina. But men can have an orgasm without an erect penis. How strange and useless will seem all the handbooks on sex when we realize that intercourse is no more complex than blowing our nose and the mystery about intercourse was only intended to restrict our pleasure so that we could go about our business of building civilizations that kept men busy so that they would not have to face their childish fears of being alone in the universe. The Pyramid at Giza is only a frightened Egyptian king crying out to some unknown god, "Look at what I can do!" But the gods never listen. No Chinese god ever strolled along the Great Wall of China. No Indian god ever spent a night in the Taj Mahal. No Protestant god ever spent an evening with the Rockefellers in their Westchester estate. Our monuments fail to appease our gods. The one monument all men have, their incredible tool, that the Japanese draw ten times its size, that the artists at Pompeii molded into gigantic spears, that the Romans made meek and limp in Florence, that stands triumphant on top of every church, a monument the primitive tribes never tired of carving out of stone, that limp monument Philip put back into his trousers and zipped up before returning below deck to curl up in the berth in the bow of the *Sea Islander.*

I stayed on deck until the dampness drove me to the warmth of the galley. I poured myself a glass of red wine and sipped the wine. Michael was asleep.

We had finished our first day at sea. Not a word was said between us. The sea is not yet into us. When the sea enters us we will become like the sea and maybe we will realize that we are not as alone as we imagine ourselves to be.

Philip's Log

I am not Herman Melville. I cannot invent a chase after a white whale. I am not Joseph Conrad. I cannot pretend there is a grand mystery to the human soul. I am not Sigmund Freud, adrift in the sea of unconsciousness. I feel there is only silence. There is no one to help me. I didn't dare tell any of my friends what happened between Elaine and Michael. What could they say to me in return? There is no one in the world who has any knowledge of the act, knowledge that would make me stop trying to understand what happened. This voyage is nothing but a voyage into the unknown. How far the voyage will take us I don't know. Perhaps it might be best for us to sail past Block Island and go into the deep Atlantic like the Russells almost did. But the Atlantic wouldn't bring us any closer to understanding. It is understanding I want. Not revenge. Revenge would be simple. I could call

Max Appleson and have him start a divorce proceeding in five minutes. I could strip Elaine of alimony payments, her interest in the house, her interest in any of my possessions. Any judge would cast her into the wilderness the way the Puritans used to cast offenders into the wilderness, to starve or be killed by the Indians. The Puritans never showed mercy. To offend was to remove yourself. How long the rule of the Puritans has lasted. For Elaine's offense they would have burned her at the stake, but even the flames might not have been enough. They would have ground up her scorched bones and mixed the ashes with the excrement of a pig and thrown the whole mess into another fire to be purified.

I have no words for this log. Human speech misses so much. We have invented words to conceal ourselves from one another. How long it takes us to be accurate about our feelings. I have no precise language for what I feel. I would like to state in this log just how I feel but I find the words escape me. Let me make one more effort. A ship's log must be accurate.

I came home from work. I walked from the Larchmont station to our house. That walk took about twenty minutes. I went into our house. I walked up the stairs to see Michael. I opened the door. I saw Michael on the bed. I saw my wife on top of Michael. I stood there for an instant unable to move. Then I dragged Elaine off my son. I struck my wife. I called her all kinds of names. She cried. She fought back. Michael didn't say a word, he didn't move. That night we slept in different beds. I picked up the telephone a dozen times to call Max Appleson to tell him to get a divorce letter in the mail that night. I didn't talk to Max

Appleson. I didn't pack a bag and leave the house. I stayed home. I couldn't sleep. I tossed and turned and tried to find a language for my feelings, but I had no feeling other than an anger that wouldn't leave me. If I had found Elaine with another man, that would have been easy. I would have called Max Appleson and the divorce letter would have been in the morning mail. I would have run from the adultery and sought the quickest divorce. But her incest with Michael is something different. I feel I must find an explanation for the incest, carry away an understanding, and that the explanation must come from the three of us, Elaine, Michael, myself.

I am less nervous on the boat. I don't tremble. I don't feel the earth slipping away underneath me. The three vodka martinis have helped. The moon is full and lights up the water. Elaine is on the upper deck. What if I had stayed in the office. If I hadn't come home early. What would have happened between Michael and Elaine. Would she have gotten out of bed as she does with me, reach for the Kleenex, wipe herself, go into the john, rinse her hands, light a cigarette, sit down in front of the lighted mirror and stare at her face, and then turn to Michael and ask how he was doing in his English class? What did she *do?* She took a muscle of her son's body, took it when it was erect, placed the muscle inside of her, for that is the way she mounts me—she says all the drawings in Pompeii show the woman on top—and then she rode up and down on the muscle, the way the painted horses go up and down on a merry-go-round, and then she shuddered, and that was the end of it. There is no mystery to the sexual act except we always approach it as though we are doing it for the first time and for me the act has long since lost its wonder. I don't think I enter Elaine more than once a week, and each time there is less and less excitement for me even though I cannot rid myself of the thought that the act must be magical, otherwise why would we attribute so much to it, and why would millions upon millions of people perform it as though the entire world was watching them each time.

Shakespeare is silent. Moses is silent. Freud is silent. I searched the Larchmont Public Library catalog Saturday and it was silent on Elaine. Elaine on the deck looking at the stars as though she placed them there. Elaine with her silence that shrieks at you. Elaine who would rush out of the house and cast off the Blue Jay as though the Long Island Sound was the North China Sea. Elaine who I have no more made my wife than I can capture the attention of the waitresses at McDonald's. No ship's log can containe Elaine. Elaine who would leave the house at ten, eleven at night, and I thought she was taking the car to Scarsdale to meet a man in one of those bars on Central Avenue. Instead when I followed her one night she went down to the Sound and drove in and around the wild parts of the shore that you reach through the back roads in Mamaroneck and Rye. I don't know why she married me. She should have married somebody wrapped up in a black robe who could fly and talk to animals and plants and part the waves. I've never told this to anyone until now, and now only the ship's log which I will rip up and throw into the Sound.

I have been in awe of Elaine since I married her. On the surface she is a Larchmont housewife. Neatly taking the corner of the Post Road with the Mercedes. Stopping off at Citibank. Ordering meat at the butcher's. Picking out grapefruit at Gristede's. Dropping off old clothes at the Golden Shoestring for the Junior League ladies to sell. Taking the Blue Jay out alone. Using the ten-speed Raleigh when she doesn't feel like driving the Mercedes. Picking up the *New Yorker* at the Corner Store. Going to the teas at the Larchmont Public Library because she once worked for a publisher and is on the mailing list for the authors' and publishers' Sunday afternoons in May. Giving fifty dollars to the Larchmont Volunteer Fire Department in case we ever need them. Making all the parents' nights at school. Driving to Presbyterian to see her gynecologist. Taking clothes on Saturday morning to Matt's for cleaning. Within the one square mile of Larchmont she knows how to use all of the services and which merchants to gossip with if she wants a favor. It is a game all the women play in Larchmont until they slip into middle age. But underneath the surface there is a wife I have never embraced alone in bed. I always feel a third presence in bed that I cannot identify but that I can feel like a chill wind. I am never in full possession of Elaine the way I expected to be and perhaps no man ever is. I have always felt Elaine was possessed by someone else. Not another man. Not as far as I knew. But possessed by a mood I couldn't penetrate. There were times when I wanted to get rid of Elaine and find myself a more comfortable wife who would live with me into my old age and be there to hand me pills and make me a cup of hot tea. Why am I writing all this in the ship's log? This must be what every man feels about his wife. All women are elusive.

My God, how could they carry a living body in them and not be elusive. Not one woman in a billion understands that she is the carrier of life. Not one woman in a billion understands the life she carries in her for nine months. Women are not elusive the way we imagine them to be, elusive with some kind of marvelous power of prophecy or understanding. Women are elusive because they do not understand their bodies and they look upon themselves as though viewing themselves through a mirror. Women never see themselves *in* a mirror.

Women only see the mystery in themselves. What if, what if, what if Elaine didn't see the mystery but only the practicality of herself. Maybe I have been in awe of her practicality. There is something fearful about being practical in a world built on novelty. Aren't all of our lives adjusted to the niceties of novelty? How quickly we make novelty a necessity, like wide ties or short skirts, tennis, winning the Bermuda race, perfecting oral techniques while making love manuals best sellers. Elaine took *The Joy of Sex* and burned it page by page in our fireplace when she learned it had sold three hundred thousand copies in America.

How has Elaine shown her practicality? I don't mean Elaine being practical about the price of chopped sirloin or green peppers, or running to garage sales to buy an old potato masher. Elaine has been practical about her privacy. She has been practical about the books she reads. Feeling that the critics on the *Times* have destroyed the pleasure in reading, she has found her own books in the stacks at the Larchmont Public Library—obscure books, books donated by Westchester matrons being moved from fifteen-room houses on the Sound into nursing-home beds. She has liked the kind of books they wrote in the nineteenth century, travel books, books on gardens, Indian temples, New England houses, the Dutch houses of New York, the early anthropological writings. She devoured that great book by Sumner, *Folkways,* and she delighted in the early writing of Freud when he was telling other psychiatrists how to set up their businesses. She was fascinated by a book about a Mrs. Grundy. She brought home old sailing books. She spent days reading an old book called *Sex and Religion* filled with extraordinary drawings, written by a dentist who read all the forbidden books before anyone knew they existed. Elaine has been practical about the mystery of things. She fed the birds all winter and didn't mind if the Larchmont raccoons came out of the sewers and knocked over our garbage cans for food. She was even practical with me in bed, now that I remember. She has never challenged me, never mocked me, never let me feel the act has been useless, never denied me the pleasure of feeling that I possessed her body. Yes, she has needed me for her freedom to dream, to sail, to play tennis, to cycle, read, take long walks in Manor Park, to go up to her private room on the third floor where she has always had a telescope fixed on Jupiter. I provide the income, the house, the money necessary for her to be herself. I have never questioned what kind of a mother she has been, for Michael has grown and matured. He got good marks in school and he had the easy grace of boys growing up in Larchmont, a grace which comes from money, from having your own room, seeing the great white houses on the shore, knowing famous people live around the corner, like the anchorman on ABC or a playwright who just sold a play to United Artists for $300,000. Michael has always been free and loose about girls, all of whom have had grace and beauty as though they were trained by Tiffany. Amy has been the loveliest of the girls, something like Elaine. They both seem to see with a third eye and let you know they understand more than they reveal. I am sure Amy and Michael have slept together because she has come down from his room as softly as Jennie, the cat, and looking just as wise.

Ship's log. It is time for sleep. Do children still say the Lord's Prayer? Now I lay me down to sleep, I pray the Lord my soul to keep. In that big king-sized bed of ours, Elaine and I would lie down to sleep. Elaine with her ritual of sleep. First the scrubbing of the face. Then the rinsing of clothes. Then a glance at me to see if I wanted her. If she sensed I did, she would take off her clothes in front of me, undoing her brassiere so that I would see her breasts, and that meant we had entered into an agreement to bind one another's bodies together in an act that I think proceeded and not preceded human life. Don't ask me to explain that thought. Except that I have always believed that the human act of fucking is far removed from what animals do, which is why we are incapable of understanding fucking as a simple animal act.

Ship's log? Will I sleep tonight without tossing and turning and trying to hold the world still for an instant so that I can fall asleep? Will I sleep when I slide into the long narrow berth in the front of the ship which is like a cocoon? Will I come out of the cocoon in the morning breathing the fresh sweet air of the Thimble Islands and seeing the early dawn sunlight on the water? East is Block Island. What would Elaine do if I tried to get into her berth? Why does a husband always want his wife when she doesn't want him?

Ship's log? Can you tell me why I am so calm toward Michael? Is it because I don't want to lose him? Is it because I believe he was innocent? But why didn't he throw his mother out of the room? Why didn't he guess her intentions and run for the shower?

Ship's log? Is it possible this boat can go down? Ocean liners have sunk in the Sound. Boats have vanished in the Sound. Is that my intention, to have the boat vanish in the Sound with no trace of us ever to be found, to have that mystery we share—Michael, Elaine, and myself—sink with us to the bottom of the Sound, to be anchored on the bottom throughout time, lost like the gossip aboard a Spanish man-of-war sunk in the English Channel. Is this what I want? Silence. Or, do I want an explanation from Elaine? Can any explanation explain what she did so that the three of us can live together again? I do not think so, ship's log. I think we will sail past Block Island. I think we will sail into the Atlantic. I think we will sail until we are swamped. We will go down too far out in the Atlantic for our screams to be heard. We will return to the silence of the sea where our language is useless and the words we have formed are washed away and all that remains is waiting for a trumpet call that may someday summon us to a full explanation of why we were born.

On television I saw a bird taken out of a hole in the ground in England, placed in a wooden box, put aboard a jet liner, flown to Boston where the bird was examined, its stomach painted blue, and then let loose on the coast of Massachusetts. The bird flew across the Atlantic Ocean and was found in the same hole where it had been taken for its flight to Boston. For fourteen days the bird traveled across the Atlantic searching for its home. What does the flight of the bird with the painted blue stomach tell us? Ship's log, you know the answer. We all want to make landfall. Landfall. There you see land rising out of the sea. Landfall. All the sailors rushing to the ship's rail, a point of land found by a compass, the stars, the sails. How incredible that a ship can find the spot of land it is searching for on the great body of water that is always a horizon.

The Sound

The sky was gray, overcast, the water looked like lead, swells rose and fell, the sea gulls cackled and headed for land where they would eat the remains from the barbecue pits. Michael put on his foul-weather jacket and foul-weather pants. Elaine wore a foul-weather jacket over a heavy fisherman's sweater. Philip wore his sweater with oiled wool, denim shorts. The rain Philip dreaded would come at any minute. He didn't want to fight the weather, he wanted to fight Elaine, who had remained in her berth until the boat was under way. She hadn't gotten up to prepare breakfast. Philip and Michael had had orange juice and cold cereal. A hot cup of coffee would have been a delight.

In the middle of the night Philip could no longer sleep in the tight narrow berth and crawled out to be near Elaine. He thought she wouldn't resist but she did. He slipped into the berth next to her, careful not to make a sound, but when he touched her she whispered into his ear, "Get out," in a voice as cold as the wind that cut across the open boat. He got out of Elaine's berth and tossed in his own berth until he awoke and saw the gray sky and heard the mournful cry of the birds who assembled on the rocks of the Thimble Islands like a Greek chorus. He had awakened to gray mornings on Block Island, when the entire island looked like it would sink into the Atlantic, but then the sun had come out, the birds had sung more sweetly, and the cyclists had begun heading for the cliffs.

The sun would come out today. He gave orders for Michael to cast off. They swung into the Sound. Their heading was due east for Block Island. Then the sun vanished as though it would never appear again. Elaine came out on deck and said, "Why did you cast off in this foul weather? We're in no hurry to get to Block Island. Can't you see the storm approaching?"

"No. We can head back to the Thimble Islands or try to run for Fisher's Island. We're not that far from land if real trouble should break."

"You're always in trouble on the Sound if a storm breaks," Elaine said, "no matter how close you are to the land."

"Do you want to turn back?"

"We'll go on toward Block Island. Maybe you're right, the storm may break clean, suddenly. It looks like that kind of day."

The *Sea Islander* rose with the waves and sank with the waves. The swells burst up against the boat. The bailer was working, otherwise the deck would have been swamped.

Michael held the boat on course for Block Island.

They had been in storms before. He knew there would be a storm before they got to Block Island. But he didn't expect the storm until they left the Sound and entered the open waters of the Atlantic where no mercy was shown to any boat. He braced his feet against the swells that rocked the boat. It was easy to be washed overboard if you lost your balance. The Connecticut shore was no comfort now. It was lost in the gray haze. When a storm struck the Sound you no longer believed that people lived in comfortable houses on the shore close by, that the color TV set was going and the kitchens were filled with the smell of frying bacon and hot coffee. You no longer wondered why you were on the water when you could drive to New London in two hours and take the ferry to Block Island. You were on the water and that was all that counted. You couldn't think about anything else because if a wave came at the boat and you weren't prepared for it the boat could go under, no matter how much ballast it carried or what guarantees you'd gotten from the boatyard in Mamaroneck.

The rain struck him across the face like a slap. It came in sheets of driving downpour. The sky was black. A bolt of lightning hit the sky. The wind howled. His father came on deck with two life jackets.

"We'd better put these on," his father said. "Let me take the helm. We'll try to ride out the storm."

"It's a typical Long Island Sound storm," Michael said, yelling into the wind. "I've been out in one of these off Larchmont."

"This is a storm in the Atlantic. You get different kinds of swells. I don't know if this boat can really take an Atlantic storm."

"Block Island isn't the real Atlantic," Michael said.

"It's fourteen miles into the Atlantic. That's enough to make it the real Atlantic. We're riding these swells all right. There's nothing to worry about. We're just getting wet."

"It looks like it may break up," Michael said.

"You're right. The storms last a few minutes this time of year. But you have to be ready for them. Look at the sky," Philip said to his son, "those black clouds are breaking up. We're going to get a brilliant sky in a few minutes. The rain will stop. We'll wonder why we were worried. We'll wonder where the storm came from. I don't think this storm held us up for Block Island. We should make landfall around five or six."

The storm didn't let up. The wind tore against the boat as though it wanted every obstacle in its way overturned. The sky was black. Philip hung on to the tiller to keep the boat from floundering. Michael tied a rope around himself and his father in case one of them was washed overboard. Elaine remained in the cabin holding on to the overhead supports as the boat swung crazily from side to side.

Elaine could see the ocean smash against the plastic windows of the galley. She knew storms didn't last forever. It was a case of holding on until the storm let up. She had been in storms with the Blue Jay. But nothing like this wild outburst of nature that flung the water of the Sound into the air and broke the waves over the boat. Why did the Sound get so furious? Why was it necessary for there to be storms at sea? What did a storm at sea mean? Was it to stir up the bottom of the sea? Was this the way nature incubated new life at the bottom of the sea, calmly waiting for millions of centuries to pass, for billions of storms, before new forms of life started to walk out of the sea. She knew they wouldn't sink. The *Sea Islander* could be turned over on its side in the water, but it wouldn't sink. It was unsinkable. Or so they had been promised. The boat had never been put to a real test. She held on to the overhead supports, polished brackets of mahogany, a sensible idea. The waves smashed against the galley. The stove was swinging wildly in its gimbals. She and Philip once crossed the English Channel in a storm that flung their liner from side to side as though they were on a ride at Coney Island. She remembered the English fishing boats swamped by the waves. A huge wave would pass directly over the smaller boats, hiding them, and then the waves washed clean. The boats dipped into the water as though they were going down head first but they always reared upward. They were heavy fishing boats designed like peasant women. They must have been through a hundred storms in the Channel.

The blackness in the sky meant it could burst with a light. That was the way it was on the Sound. Once she raced the black clouds to the Larchmont shore, the wind at her back, the sails full. She could see boats behind her being swamped in the Sound but she was racing ahead of the storm, and just as she swept into Larchmont harbor the storm broke over her head and the rain poured down faster than she could bail the Blue Jay. Then suddenly the storm fled like a frightened bird.

She was never afraid on the water. Who were the men who sailed out of New Bedford on whaling voyages leaving their families for two and three years, living all that time on their great sailing ships? And without women, for the whaling ships didn't carry troop followers and no novelist or historian she had ever read suggested the men made love to one another in the hidden decks of the whaling ships, though some of the men must have caressed one another in the Indian Ocean. Philip had wanted to get into her berth at 3:30 in the morning. She had looked at her watch as he tried not to make any noise. "Get out," she had whispered in his ear.

What a strange man her husband was. Did he think she would ever sleep with him again until Michael had been thoroughly exorcised from her, deep within her, from every one of those thousands of nerve endings Michael had touched when he was in her, leaving his mark in her? For while men dared to climb Mount Everest and race in cars that went around in a circle at two hundred miles an hour, she had dared to take her son into her embrace, and that single act was enough to make even the men who climbed Mount Everest tremble with horror. She knew Philip wanted to penetrate her to see if he could feel anything of Michael in her, that was the trinity the church had been talking about for two thousand years, which the church understood but its worshipers didn't dare understand except in hidden moments when fathers and daughters or brothers and sisters discovered one another's bodies as innocently as two cats playing together in a backyard. Almost everyone looked with horror on such knowledge between a mother and son —though their embrace would seem to be the most natural act in the world—if only because children live in so much fear of its consequence, as though it would swallow them up and return them to the silence of the womb. How stupid we are with our lives. How little grace we have. A squirrel sitting on its haunches eating a chestnut has grace. We never forget the bad lessons of our childhood. Men more than women, because men have more toys to play with, men never get out of their childhood. Women would like to go beyond their parents. Men only want to be patted on the head, given a title or a ribbon. Didn't Napoleon once say he could take 700,000 lives for a blue ribbon, a million for a red ribbon? Women know they give birth. How great the name midwife. Midwife. Babies should never be delivered by male doctors. They give the newborn baby the vibrations of fear.

The storm would end. They would sit down on the deck and sort out their lives. This is what we are. Life.

Six

The Whirlwind

I cleared the storm. God can do anything. Except I
cannot bend human life as I can the branch of a tree
or the crest of a wave. I can summon a storm at sea,
but I cannot make a person take one more step forward or one more step backward than he chooses to
make.

I can watch. I can listen. I can descend like some
great novelist on a single life and try to understand
that life and be no more successful than the great
novelist who must surrender to bewilderment. But
I never give up. From where I am I see every single human life as though each life towers like the
Matterhorn. No one life escapes me. No one can hide.
No one can flee from his skin, even those unhappy
people I see who have reduced all life to a state from
which they dare not make a single move. They fear
disturbing the stability they feel they have brought to

their lives. But what chaos rages in their minds, how invisible their fears.

I am always willing to learn. Man is the only form of life I can learn from. Because man invents his own history. I have nothing to do with the history of man, though I have observed it from its very beginning. Even I do not understand how it happened that man came to think about his own existence. All the activity I see on earth from actors on stages talking to audiences and singers marching in grand processions and men filling books with ideas, and all the stately statues that stand in every corner of the world, and the paintings that seize on human life as though there is a way of freeing life from itself, all those grand works that exist in every corner of the earth and even in caves hidden from the sunlight, all are man-made, although men like to think they have their origin in me.

I am now interested in the three people on the *Sea Islander* who have passed through the storm on Long Island Sound, sailing alone in sight of more than eighteen million people who live within a half-hour's drive of the Sound, the most highly skilled and learned people on the face of the earth, yet who tremble at the sight of themselves and do not believe their own lives.

Why is my gaze on the sailing boat? I never tire of learning. The wife and the mother must now tell the husband and father what he does not dare to hear but which he cannot dare not to hear. The son must listen too. The three have created a marvel that is life. Neither I nor anyone else on earth is wise enough to tell them what they must do. They must decide for themselves on the boat, the *Sea Islander,* now under full sail, catching a fast wind, with the sun appearing out of the dark clouds like a bride who advances triumphantly to meet her husband.

It is one of the most beautiful sights on earth. A sailboat with its white sails fully catching the wind, the blue sky, the green water of its sea. The horizon is where the water and the sky meet. And on such oceans, I can tell you, great continents of land like North America have floated and shifted like lilies in a pond.

I will tell no one I am aboard. The wind is carrying the *Sea Islander* toward Block Island. But I want to see the landfall Elaine is going to make, Elaine who I first noticed when she peered over my shoulder and looked at sights denied to Moses.

Sea Islander

Elaine took the tiller. Philip and Michael were exhausted from the storm. The sun was out. Here and there whitecaps reminded them of the storm. But the whitecaps were disappearing under the warmth of the sun and a wind that was now a whisper.

Coming through storms in the Sound was like awakening from a dream that threatened to disturb your sleep forever. How often Elaine had longed to hang on to the tail of a dream and stay with the dream until it returned back to where it had begun. Certainly dreams have an older life than the bodies they inhabit. Dreams must be messages from another planet. How often she had thought of this planet as merely a testing ground for other worlds. Something like the Olympic trials. But who knew what kind of person was needed to live again on the worlds that used dreams as their messages. Maybe this was the reason we were all so different, yet so alike, and why the time-honored among us were beginning to crumble, afraid to hear new messages. When she was a girl a judge was never arrested, a governor was never indicted, a Vice-President was beyond suspicion, and a President somehow filled his office. Now that was over. For her it meant that a new round of testing was beginning and new types of men would emerge and perhaps even women would begin to find themselves suspect. Women had a curious habit of always believing they were right. The Frenchman put it another way: All men believe they are right when they kill. The world was breaking up into new jigsaw pieces. She had no doubt of that; everyone wondered why the old pieces didn't fit.

Ahead, east, past the Race they had sailed through, that turbulent body of water in the Sound leading into the Atlantic, were the headwaters of eternity. That phrase from Melville had thrilled her as a girl when she read *Moby Dick* tightly curled up in a wing chair before a blazing fire, where she guessed what Melville was trying to do, to be greater than Shakespeare as an American, and to pour on America his holy words as though he could slow down the headlong dash of Americans toward profit and loss as the instruments of all existence. Melville failed and the critics failed his book and *Moby Dick* was left to float in the great oceans like a bottle filled with a message from the gods.

She had grown up believing in the giants of literature just as the Greeks believed in their variety of gods. In a moment of despair there was always Proust trying to recall memories that not even Proust could replace with words. When she despaired of justice there was Camus rising out of the war like Apollo. There were moments when Fitzgerald satisfied her. But she always returned to Melville and Henry Adams. Between them they held her world together, and none of the literary snipers could fool her, for the snipers were doomed men, like the German snipers who were tied to trees in the movies she saw of World War I.

She never knew when she passed from the safety of her gods, her books, those great writers who spoke directly to her as though they were whispering into her ear, to the isolation of herself. It may have begun when she took the Blue Jay out on that afternoon that now seemed as long ago as an evening in Thebes. No, it had to be before that afternoon, for the mind is always evolving, always in defense of itself, one never takes an action until the mind gives a clear signal.

The headwaters of eternity were ahead of them. The *Sea Islander* was heading into the open waters of the Atlantic. The swells were longer, the water greener. Two-thirds of the earth was covered with water. The *Sea Islander* was a speck on the water, a bare thirty-one feet, and the Atlantic, at any moment it chose, could cast the *Sea Islander* on her side and tear the mast from its rigging as one snaps a toothpick. She had always been frightened of the Atlantic, she had lived through two storms on it from which she had thought she would not escape alive. Her fear was of the immensity of the Atlantic, of invading a world beyond her imagination, a world inhabited by billions of fish created in millions of shapes and colors, until one could no longer imagine what was in the mind of God when he undertook such a creation, unless he was endlessly experimenting, and to what purpose no one could guess.

The endless sea of her husband Philip and her son Michael was before her. They were both on deck. Philip stared over the bow as though prehistoric monsters lurked ahead of them. Michael would look up from time to time to smile at her, as though he should be shown mercy. It was time to turn the *Sea Islander* into the headwaters of eternity. The sun was out in its glory. The sea caught its glow. There were no other boats in sight, no forty-foot powerboats bearing down on them from Greenwich, no fleets of sail. Just a sky that was the same sky under which Moses walked, Homer, Horace, Euripides, Alexander, Galileo. They could all rise from their sleep and recognize the world they had left and carry on the conversations that had been interrupted.

It was time to begin her defense.

The sea was her courtroom. In the waves and swells she could see the jury. Above her was the dome of the sky which the Greeks once thought was supported by great columns, even if no one ever saw the columns. Homer believed the world was limited to his vision. She was no Homer and she could only begin by addressing her husband.

"Philip." Philip turned at the sound of her voice as though he had been ordered to begin the ascent to the top of the gallows he had always seen as his fate. "Michael." Michael stopped pretending to be on the lookout for lobster pots. "I can't talk against the wind. So please come a little closer."

Philip moved up from the bow. Michael turned from the ocean to look at his mother.

"I don't want either of you to interrupt me. In a courtroom both the prosecuting attorney and the defense attorney are allowed to speak uninterrupted when they begin their summation. The great trials always leave us a little baffled. Who was guilty? Was guilt proven? Who did steal the Lindbergh baby? Were the Rosenbergs ready to betray America to atomic dust? Was Patty Hearst a bank robber? Why did Leopold and Loeb kill? Did Socrates corrupt the youth of Athens? We have invented laws to protect us. We have invented our own history to prove that we are innocent. Marriage makes beasts of husbands and wives. In America we permitted children to drag cars full of coal fifteen hundred feet underground because children were cheaper than donkeys. We still destroy life in America as casually as we kill a housefly. Count the people in mental institutions, the suicides among children, the retarded who have been brain damaged by their environment, the people killed on the highways because we have made the automobile more important than our lives."

Were the waves listening? Had she begun on the right note? Would the great white whale carry her words to the Indian Ocean? No one would listen to her on the shores washed by the Atlantic. Her crime was too great. The horror too well implanted. The *Sea Islander* was drifting. She brought the boat back on course. For the Greeks there were only the great rivers at the edge of the world. The compass brought the world together under one sky. She had been five degrees off course, enough for them to miss Block Island. It was not the right beginning. She could not appeal to history. There was no history for what she had done, only horror, drifting across the centuries like a great gray cloud that kept people indoors.

No, that was not the beginning to take. She had not spoken aloud but only to herself, as she had for days and weeks and years, keeping to herself her thoughts, as though waiting for new sounds to appear in human speech, sounds that would make her understandable to someone other than herself. She was not the first person to catch glimpses of other worlds, and she would not be the last. But how should she begin when history preceded her and preempted all her arguments? She was on trial for sleeping with her son, only that, and not for murdering her father, which the Greeks considered a greater crime.

When she was a little girl her entire family would sit and talk in the kitchen on Friday nights and give one another comfort. They were all released from the need to conceal themselves from one another. Her father would complain that he wanted to be a doctor, but the Depression had forced him into taking a civil service job for which he was overqualified and the dream of his life was to buy an old Revolutionary War house and live in it like some elder statesman busy writing his memoirs.

Her mother died before they could move into the Revolutionary War house that her father eventually found in Chagrin Falls, Ohio. Her father used to tell her, "You have to forget my love because it is not enough to sustain you in this world, it's enough to sustain me only, and it will hurt you more than help you." How did her father know that? How did her father know that a parent's affection goes on and on year after year, and after a time it is all he may cling to. The worst of parents never want their children to leave them. They hunt after them all of their lives, never daring to kill them, just wounding them. The parents play the game of love, tantalizing their children with affection and then withholding love, and the children spend the rest of their days like epic wanderers looking for that which cannot be found anywhere else except in their parents.

Someday, she hoped, psychiatrists would see beyond the Oedipal. But who would listen to her? She had the credentials of a Larchmont housewife who played tennis and drove a Mercedes to the Club where she kept her Blue Jay. If she could save her son, she could afford to lose something of her own life. She would not howl for comfort, as some of the wives she knew in Larchmont, nor would she consider suicide, which was a child's resolution. She was a woman, that much she knew of herself, and being a woman for her was more than the right to open a charge account at Bloomingdale's in her own name. A woman, she knew, was nothing more or less than the universe compressed into a human form. This is what all true artists have seen and why the Virgin Mary has persisted in a world that has hunted virgins down as if they were debtors.

Elaine's Story

Let us imagine, Elaine began, that we are on a voyage with no landfall. We made our departure from the Larchmont shoreline but we have no landfall in sight. It is not Block Island we are seeking but another land-fall that we have no map for, no compass reading, no charts. Before that we are in our house in Larchmont. We sit at supper without daring to look at one another. At night we go into separate bedrooms. In the morning Philip flees to his office without eating breakfast. Michael, you run out of the house to see Amy and you try to return when you think we are asleep. I'm glad you have Amy to comfort you. She seems to me to be a very wise girl. There is something wild and wonderful about her and I am sure she knows more than she reveals to anyone except possibly you. I was a little like Amy when I was a girl. I was always reading, always asking questions of the authors I read, and I considered most of them closer to me than anyone else I knew. I would quarrel with Dostoevski. I would lose my patience with Tolstoy, he seemed to understand everything except the mystery of life. I loved Charles Dickens, Nathaniel Hawthorne, and Herman Melville. I did not believe that any man could have written *Hamlet* until I realized that Shakespeare was just writing in the language his audience wanted to hear and he asked the questions they wanted to hear while answering nothing of substance. Shakespeare was the great asker of the human question, wasn't he? Shakespeare was not very profound. He just had a good memory. I loved the poets. Tennyson was glorious, Milton, Wordsworth, all the Englishmen. Poets are the children of the human race. Do you remember Tennyson's "The Two Voices," Michael? You were reading Tennyson last month in school. "Moreover, something is or seems/ That touches me with mystic gleams,/Like glimpses of forgotten dreams—/Of something felt, like something here;/ Of something done, I know not where;/ Such as no language may declare." That was Tennyson. We are going to talk about things "such as no language may declare." I'll begin with myself, the way I felt last Friday morning.

I was going to go into New York City to see my hairdresser to get my hair cut when I decided I would rather take the Blue Jay out. Maybe I should have gone in to have my hair cut when I decided I would rather take the Blue Jay out. Maybe I should have gone in to have my hair cut at Mergad's like all the models in *Vogue*. A short haircut would help my tennis. Isn't tennis the most important activity in Larchmont? I didn't go into New York City. I stayed in Larchmont and took out the Blue Jay.

I had no plan in mind. I just wanted to sail for an hour or two. It looked like a good day for sailing. I like to sail alone. I find the water friendly. I find the water makes it possible for me to live in Larchmont. I have wanted to run from Larchmont for years. This is a community of tragedy. The tragedy stays hidden. It never surfaces. But tragedy is the face of Larchmont. Didn't Mr. Burton down the street from us hang himself in his garage? Didn't a friend of yours, Michael, take his mother's sleeping pills and swallow the whole bottle of pills? Didn't Mrs. Gertz walk down to Manor Park, take off her shoes and stockings like a little girl going wading in a puddle, and drown herself? That's three suicides we know about. How many suicides didn't get into the Larchmont paper? I know what suicide is. It is when a person pulls out all the plugs and doesn't let any messages come in. A suicide hears nothing but his own voice telling him to die. That is what is happening to us today. We don't hear the incoming messages. We are afraid to listen. We fear the news we have to tell one another. We no longer live in the safety of our kitchen. My God, how I miss my father and my mother telling us about their days in Ohio and the Depression and the way they lived then. As crazy as it may look in the old newsreels on Channel 13, it was still life. Now we prefer to kill ourselves rather than pick up a telephone and say we are sorry or stupid or afraid. We have forced on psychiatrists a wisdom they don't possess, which none of them have the courage to admit. We are told in the newspaper that President Nixon wanted to drop atomic bombs like coconuts. He walked around the

White House drunk and didn't sleep with his wife for fourteen years and she didn't have the courage to tell the world that he was a madman in the White House.

What does all of this have to do with us? We are spared nothing. In the old world only a handful of people knew what was going on at any one time. Maybe the editors of the *Times,* some journalists, a few politicians, a few writers, maybe a novelist like Orwell or Camus. But today we each know every day the horror that develops from the previous day's horror. We see unrelenting horror each day. We feel helpless. We feel ready to surrender. We don't know who to surrender to. But don't worry, the day will come soon when someone or other will tell us that he is the person we must surrender to and we will do it happily like the victim in *1984,* only sooner and with more joy. We all long for a kind of long-promised joy, a reward for being alive, a promise from some ancient gods that we will be given a bag full of goodies. We believe that this is our due on this earth and we wait forever for the joy that we feel ought to be given to us. I think I have discovered what this joy is and why it exists and why it is never given and why it is foolish for us to continue to believe in it while the world changes every morning, turning us into the most frightened creatures on earth.

I wish I was someone more important, some professor at Oxford or Harvard, Yale, Columbia, MIT, or any one of the schools that we think feed us wisdom. We believe so much in credentials. We believe no one who doesn't have credentials. We are afraid to believe in ourselves. We run to the experts and the experts run to bourbon and suicide for their solutions. What is it that I think I know?

What I think I know affects the three of us. If we can believe it I will be happy. If we can't believe it then we will not be spared. If the rest of the world believes it, fine, but I don't know how to tell the rest of the world, and in time the world will find out. The secret has been kept long enough.

I am aware of the two experiences that affect every single person in the years he is growing up. The one experience I have called childhood amnesia, which we have talked about, Philip, which I didn't invent or discover, that was done by other people who have been ignored in the history of science. I came across the concept when I started teaching school. Childhood amnesia simply means that there is a period in everyone's life which he can't recall, which dates from his earliest and often happiest years. They are the years from birth until the child begins to develop the memory he must have to get along in the culture he lives in. Before the child develops his second memory it is necessary for society to wipe out the first memory. The destruction of that first memory is done through what is taught in school, at home, the street, and all the information that is fed to the growing child. The child learns what it is important for him to remember. Society can't tolerate a really free spirit. That free spirit would be a challenge to everyone and everything. Other people might say, "Why can't we be free, why can't we return to those days we can't remember but which remain in us like a hum in an automobile we can't locate." This is one of the golden periods of human life. The period before we lose our first memory. The memory that we are born with. The memory that gives us our first view of the sun, the sky, birds, the faces of our parents, flowers, water, trees, music, the magic movement of day and night, the stars, the music of the heavens, the bright beautiful colors, the shapes of things we can't name. Nothing in our first memory has a name. It is all color, light, music, move-ment, shapes, sounds, a dazzling feeling of complete identity with the universe. Nothing is strange. Nothing is foreign.

We can't live with that kind of dazzling memory. All societies have learned that they must wipe out that memory if people are to work, to be busy, to make objects, to conform, to believe what is told them, to obey, to die if necessary, to be beasts of burden, to suffer, to live as though they have no right to live. This is the job of education, to wipe out the childhood memory, to replace that memory with a new memory. But all of our lives we hear the music of that first memory and we long to return to it. This is what art is. Artists try to find that childhood memory and the best of them succeed. They are the artists who touch us most deeply. Who communicate most directly with us. Whose fame lasts and lasts. This is the artist in all of us, the longing to return to that first memory that gave us so much joy and which nothing can completely drive out of our minds. It is the pull of this memory that forces us to find out more and more about our-selves and that returns night after night in our dreams. It is the source of our unhappiness. It affects most deeply those people who cannot push ahead in this world, who long for a prior existence as a way of es-cape and who are led to believe they can find this escape through all kinds of inventions from drugs to standing on their heads. This is the reason why people flock to false messiahs, to spiritual leaders, to saviors who promise them a return to the joy they once experienced, a joy that is useless in dealing with the demands of our existence. If we were only floating objects in space, that kind of joy could go on and on. But the earth is something that must be worked. We are not animals who find our world laid out in neat boundaries like the aisles in a supermarket.

This amnesia was not only limited to the childhood memory. The world itself forgot why it wiped out the childhood memory and in doing so it left an empty hole in the human experience that nothing could fill except a ceaseless longing like Sisyphus trying to roll a stone up the hill. Maybe the world was afraid to tell its inhabitants that there was or is a dazzling period in the life of each one of us that is more inventive than any art the Metropolitan Museum holds under its roof. We might run like wild beasts to return to our childhood and leave the world unguarded. That is one discovery I made. Now to the second.

She knew she couldn't tell Philip and Michael everything she knew because then even her own heart would burst. Perhaps it was better to remain silent, as history had remained silent, as though it had taken a blood oath at the dawn of time. Silence would mean a divorce, leaving Larchmont, perhaps buying a cooperative on the newly built Roosevelt Island on land once called Welfare Island in the midst of the East River looking at the broad, spired belly of Manhattan, a city she detested but where else could she live with what she knew? Anonymity was the only blessing New York offered to its citizens. If one was not afraid of dying alone in the city then the anonymity was a protective cloak that spared you from revealing yourself. But she didn't want a divorce, for that would cut her off from the life she started in Michael. She knew that Philip was inter-changeable as a husband, but not Michael as a son. Michael had come out of her in the most awesome event nature permits us to witness. She had been alert, awake, all feeling, tingling, when the drama began, when Michael began to assert his right to live independent of her and like some great actor who has the stage all to himself began that epic flight all alone, daring to give up his dependence on her, that perfect world in which he floated like the planets in the universe, to come head first, all bloody and struggling like a kitten dropped to the floor, to land on his own feet and howl his arrival to the world in a cry she would never forget. She knew then that all the people who said it was a cry of defeat and fear were themselves defeated and fearful. It was a cry of life. An arrival. The deepest mystery of the universe made visible. The beginning of a new life.

Now she set the timer, as she set the timer on her kitchen counter, to make her point and no more, for she could almost see the dim long hump of Block Island. Once on Block Island they would again be what they were on land, kings, queens, knights, bishops, pawns, who knew the rules, who believed entrapment was victory.

I am going to tell you a story. When I was a little girl my father would often tell me stories. He made them up on the spur of the moment, always thinking that one day he would write them down in a book and make a million dollars and live in the Revolutionary War house he always dreamed of owning. He would make the teakettle come alive, the pots and pans, brooms, the mirrors.

In the very beginning of the world about which we know very little, but at which we can guess, I think it was quite obvious that a father, a mother, and their children had to live together. How could they live otherwise? The mother had to feed her children. The father and mother had to find food. Between them they felt the need to stay alive. The first message the brain sends to itself is to stay alive. As we get older that message gets dimmer and dimmer and in some circumstances the message is lost altogether and people kill themselves. This is how suicide is possible. The messages stop coming into the mind. When this happens the person is bewildered, he feels abandoned, and he seeks death.

In the very beginning of the world the family was the way we lived before anyone had a conception of family. The family was natural and survival was natural, no matter how dangerous the world was to the family. The very first families looked to one another for warmth, for love, for a mirror of their affection. Animals do not seem to demand the affection people do. But look at the way our Jennie bestows her affection on us, crawling into our laps when we are watching TV, leaping silently into our beds and sleeping at the foot of the bed, appearing out of nowhere to be at our side, and sometimes, just sometimes, her eyes seem to well up with a passionate longing for affection that is almost unbearable to witness. That is the way it is with us.

In the very beginning of the world the family must have lived very much alone. Here and there, in different corners of the world, families of two, three, four persons, sleeping in a cave, under trees, stacking branches together to keep out the rain. It had to be that way. It could not have been any other way.

In this family the son saw his father (not knowing he was his father) take his mother and lie on top of her for affection, and he saw them enter one another in a way that was complete. The son could witness the change in their bodies and faces as they made love. But then it must have meant something else. A delicious warmth long before the discovery of how to make fire. The son and the daughter watched this act. When they grew older they participated in the act. The son with his mother. The daughter with her father. The brother with his sister. How could it have been otherwise? From the very beginning of time it was known that this act brought warmth, an extraordinary feeling of comfort unobtainable elsewhere in the hostile world. The only comfort in the hostile world was obtainable from within your family.

Do you get a feel of what I am saying? I am trying to tell it as simply as my father told his tales to us around our kitchen table. The son knew he was entering his mother for warmth. The daughter lay under her father for warmth. Obviously the mother, the father, son, the daughter, had no notions of sex as we have, their minds were not filled with a million years of deliberate bewilderment about the most simple act two people can engage in, and they certainly had no need for directions from *Cosmopolitan* magazine. They sought one another for warmth and comfort, and that warmth and comfort were as close as their bodies that huddled together in a world that we can no longer even imagine.

But there came a time, as storytellers use the phrase, when the family huddling alone began to move toward other families. Now there were strangers. The families saw that two families could help one another bring in food, fight the animals, keep out the rain. A natural jealousy may have arisen when a father saw another man sleep with his daughter or a mother saw her son on top of another woman. Perhaps it began to dawn on the families that they could not live again as they had when they got warmth and comfort from one another. Please don't ask me how I know these things. I am guessing, just as we desperately guess that there is a purpose to our lives. I need only the proof that I believe.

There is no scientific explanation to what I am saying because this all happened long before science created its own language. I can only dare to guess because having done what I did I have the right to guess.

I think now the storyteller would say that it was obvious that the father, the mother, the son, and the daughter would no longer be able to find comfort from one another because they had new jobs to do. The father had to hunt. The mother to work. The son to hunt. The daughter to work. If one found comfort and warmth so close, why go out into a hostile world? The men in that time for which we have no record did go out into the hostile world, and the world changed. We have seen the world change from time to time. The world changed when we discovered the wheel, fire, gunpowder, the compass, machinery, electricity, atomic power. The world changed when people gave up the warmth and comfort they got from sleeping with one another within their own family. But the world has never forgotten the warmth and comfort that existed in that intimate embrace, and that is the second golden period we cannot drive out of our minds.

For this is what I think happened. Men began to say to one another, How will we accomplish anything if we don't sacrifice the comfort that we receive from entering the bodies that link us to one another? The son, the father, the mother and daughter. We must make this an act we will not tolerate. We must prohibit sons from sleeping with their mothers, fathers with daughters, and in this way we will recognize the world as it is and be able to deal with the world. Of course they had no language for this but they acted as if they did. The act of sleeping with your parents became prohibitive because it interfered with survival. It was a very wise decision. It was one of the decisions made almost at the dawn of human life. What was unwise was the way the decision was enforced. The prohibitions were so awesome—death, instant death—that the mind had to believe that there was some great delight being denied, otherwise why was the prohibition against the act so fearful, an act they knew to be so pleasant. For a million, two million, ten million years, who is there to say how many millions of years it took, the act between a mother and her son, a father and his daughter, became the one act which united almost the entire world in horror.

The terrible punishment kept alive the feeling that a golden delight was being denied, and if the dragon could be slain, the delight would be attainable. I think this accounts in part for the terrible feelings between parents and their children. Each feels bewildered and all are haunted by a golden period in the history of the world when the members of the family were able to give warmth and comfort to one another in a way that seems almost impossible today. I am not saying that if parents began sleeping with their children all would be beautiful. Please don't attribute that kind of misunderstanding to me. I am saying that we all believe in two golden periods that have been lost to us, the golden period in our childhood memories that vanish utterly from us and the golden period at the dawn of human life when the members of the family gave warmth and comfort to one another, mostly through sleeping with one another and finding a kind of unity for which we have invented a thousand religions as a poor substitute. The prohibitions have kept alive the feeling of denial.

There is more to the story.

In the distance was Block Island. She could see mists swirling up, way off, the banks of fog that closed off Block Island to everything but the ferryboats, who had radar and foghorns to penetrate the fog.

My father would never finish a story. He would get us all worked up in the kitchen over a pot and pan turned into a pair of explorers, and he would try to end with a moral, but sometimes he didn't have a moral. I have no moral to the story I am telling you. Please don't expect a moral or wait for a moral. We have not been able to forget the two golden periods that we believe existed long before we were born. There is very good reason for that belief. We come into a world that tells us what to believe and we accept the belief at an age when we are not in a position to question beliefs. Some of us hear other voices, and it is mostly the golden period of our childhood wiped out by amnesia that we long to return to through music, dancing, painting, poetry, in trying to recall our childhood memory. Our lives are like a long story, and we long to hear the end before the beginning.

The warmth and comfort that once existed in families that lived at the edge of time has never been forgotten even though its original purpose ended thousands of years ago. In the world we know, the world of Larchmont, the Connecticut towns on the Sound, the commuting trains, the women who put on their Bill Blass slacks to shop at the Grand Union, and the children who long for innocence as though it were a drug they could buy at Hughes Pharmacy, in this world purity is a creed, a belief, that we feel escapes us. We wonder why we are not all pure. We run to psychiatrists to achieve purity. We eat natural foods to achieve purity. We read sex manuals to find purity in the way we embrace one another. We feel our children are the purest objects of all and we are stunned when our children are not pure. This is the reason why children retreat into the world they know best, their own dreams, and leave the world behind, and this is the reason why children kill themselves in great numbers, because some children cannot handle the madness imposed on them.

What does all this have to do with me getting into bed with Michael and embracing him in a way that would make Hester Prynne's scarlet *A* seem like a papal blessing if my act were known to the residents of Larchmont, if they would take the time to care? I really don't care what anyone thinks except Michael. I am saying all this for you, Michael, and I will not repeat it ever again.

I wanted to free you, Michael, from the feeling that

there is a golden period in your life that you could return to if only the fates would open the bronze doors and let you through. It is that simple. You were in my arms the way those mothers thousands of years ago embraced their sons. I know it was no special experience for you. I could have been Amy or any of the girls in Larchmont that you may have slept with, for you were no stranger to the act.

I think this is what happens in families everywhere. Fathers and mothers lavish attention on their children from birth to a time when the affection becomes a bond they dare not let go of. We have the longest period of affection of all living things. If a child is not freed from this bond of affection, from the threat, yes, a threat, of never being able to sleep with his parents, then the child carries a burden no one would expect him to carry for long, for the child is not permitted to become an adult, but must always live in the shadow of an embrace the world has made obscene. What more can I tell you? I have tried to tell you this story as simply as I know how. Someone other than myself might spend a lifetime and a thousand volumes to tell the same story.

To say any more would only raise confusing questions for which we don't have any answers. Not real answers, because we haven't dared yet to ask real questions. I don't think I have hurt anyone by describing the two golden periods of life that we can never return to. It is foolish to long for them. I would like to think I am the mother of a new son, a mother like Homer might have dared to invent, who is willing to risk the gods and to do what she feels is right. I don't think we can tolerate men and women anymore who

---

live in the past, who have foolish dreams handed to them. The dream we ignore is so much more exciting.

So here you have your mother, Michael, in the one moment out of so many years when she put herself on trial as Dostoevski did in *The Brothers Karamazov*. How did Dostoevski end *The Brothers Karamazov*? You remember, Michael. You read that part aloud to me. "Hurrah for the Karamazovs." Will you say hurrah for your mother?

The Whirlwind

I heard Michael say, I love my mother. I love my father. I love Amy. I love Nancy trying so hard to live. I love my Blue Jay. I love the water, the clouds, and the sky. I love the storms when they come. I love our house, the large silent rooms, the afternoon light, the wood that has been touched by human hands for a hundred years. I love the way my father looks at tall buildings and the thrill he gets when he takes me to lunch in one of his favorite restaurants in New York. I love our cat Jennie who is not as aloof as she pretends to be. I love the soft wind that blows when the tide is down and Larchmont harbor looks like it is going to sleep for the night. I love it when we talk at dinner, that talk I hear nowhere else, that special talk among families that makes me feel so protected, that makes me feel I belong somehow to the whole history of the world and not just a small part of it. I love talking to Amy who is so wise, and yet listens to me as though I am as wise as she, which isn't true. I cannot imagine marrying anyone but Amy, but if I don't marry Amy she will always be my bride and I will never forget her and it isn't possible that we won't marry. Amy says the old world has slipped by us like a dream we can't recall. She says we are entering a new world where time moves faster than that which we can hold in our grasp, like our grandfathers and great-grandfathers were able to do, which made them feel they were in control of the world. I love the feeling of being alive. I must confess that I was alive when I was in my mother, that I will never forget, nor ever tell anyone, not even Amy, not even if we quarrel and I want to shock her. I will never tell anyone. But at that time in my mother I was touching the source of my life, and it was like that picture Michelangelo painted where a man's hand is trying to touch the hand of God, but the hand of God is never touched. What I touched in my mother was a comfort as grand as when she first fed me, which Amy said is remarkable that I remember, and I said to Amy, how could I forget it. Yes, I love this world if anyone asks. Will I say hurrah for you, Mother? Yes, a thousand times, with a thousand eagles flying overhead and a thousand sea gulls flying past you in a golden white cloud, and it is over, the thousand eagles have flown away and the thousand sea gulls are searching for clams in the sea, and that is what life is.

I heard Michael's thoughts. I would never let Michael know I had heard. He would want my judgment. Now Michael has judged himself. The judgment is his.

Elaine saw Michael's face, her son's face, and they both trembled, as one trembles before a great mountain, and there was nothing for them to conceal, just as a great mountain cannot hide itself.

The *Sea Islander* moved toward Block Island, the cliffs, the houses on the cliffs where families were hanging bathing suits up to dry and watching the sea. Elaine brought the *Sea Islander* into New Harbor, past the boys in outboard motorboats picking up supplies from the dock, past ships that looked as old as the sea, past the swaying masts. The old wooden hotels came closely into sight, children riding bicycles, all the motion of life I never tire of watching. They would soon be on land, that ball of earth babies make into mud patties because children know from birth they must fashion the earth in their own way, a lesson that is not entirely lost.

Elaine was careful at the tiller, careful to avoid the boys in their scooting outboard motorboats, careful to sail past the swaying ships, to move in and around the vessels in the crowded harbor, slowly, carefully, bringing the *Sea Islander* to berth, easing the mystery between the sea and the land. Philip let down the anchor. Michael lowered the sails. Elaine drank a glass of iced tea.

I watched them cast a tiny dinghy overboard and make their way to the shore. I learn, I learn, I learn. That is why people think I am so wise.